PRIESTESS
OF THE
LOST COLONY

PRIESTESS
OF THE
LOST COLONY

Brandon S. Pilcher

Open Books Press
Saint Louis, Missouri

Published by Open Books Press, USA

www.OpenBooksPress.com
info@OpenBooksPress.com

An imprint of Pen & Publish, LLC
www.PenandPublish.com
Saint Louis, Missouri
(314) 827-6567

Print ISBN: 978-1-941799-85-7
eBook ISBN: 978-1-941799-86-4

Library of Congress Control Number: 2021932095

Printed on acid-free paper.

ACHAEA
TROY
HITTITES
MYCENAE
PER-PEHU
PHOENICIA
GREAT GREEN SEA
CANAAN
HYKSOS
THE RED LAND
KEMET
WAWAT

CHAPTER ONE

1600 BC, in an alternate timeline

Itaweret moved her final pawn off the last square on the *senet* board. She straightened on her stool and crossed her arms with a triumphant smirk, victory assured in the game of passing.

"By all the gods, not again!" Bek slammed his hands on the ebony table, which knocked his two remaining pawns off the game board. "There must be some mistake!"

Itaweret laughed. "What mistake? That you've been losing the past few times? I keep telling you, Brother, you take these games much too seriously. You act as if the fate of all Per-Pehu depended on it."

Bek narrowed his eyes as his lips curled into a snarl. "I might not be wrong, then. If I am to govern this colony, I must hone my strategic skills. How can I do that when I keep losing to a—a *priestess?*"

Itaweret didn't take one grain of offense. If anything, his righteous anger amused her even more. "Remember what Father says. You do not need to succeed to learn."

Bek opened his mouth for another retort but stopped, stood from his stool beside the table, and took a deep breath. His mahogany-skinned brow sparkled with sweat from the afternoon sunlight that descended upon the back courtyard. He stormed across the courtyard to an alabaster bench beneath one of the olive trees and plopped down to sulk in its shade.

As entertaining as her brother's tantrums were at the end of every senet game, any pleasure Itaweret felt evaporated when she saw him wipe a tear off his cheek. Not since they were children had she seen Bek show such emotion unless he thought nobody was looking.

She walked over, sat beside him on the bench, and laid her arm on his shoulders. "It is alright, Brother. Take your mind off it."

She pointed to the rectangular pool in the middle of the court-yard, which was fringed with papyrus reeds, its blue lotus flowers throwing off a delectable fragrance. "Remember how you loved to chase the frogs across the lily pads? Or how you would dig every morning under the palm trees in search of treasure or old monster bones? I believe the hole is still there."

Bek brushed her arm off. "I outgrew those childish things years ago. I am a man now. And what's more, I am the great chief of Per-Pehu's son. I should be off studying anyway."

He got up and retreated quickly to the columned gallery sur-rounding the courtyard, disappearing through the doorway that led to his bedchamber.

Itaweret sighed and muttered a prayer, asking the gods to guide her younger brother to find peace in his heart. Bek looked at matters in the world differently: everything the gods had placed on earth would test his mettle as the future great chief. He even regarded the senet game as less of a diversion and more of a practice of his tactical abilities, should he have to lead the colony's garrison into battle. Not even the sons of the pharaohs back in Kemet, across the Great Green Sea to the south, would have preoccupied themselves with such uneasy anticipation of their responsibilities.

Itaweret couldn't do more to ease her poor brother's temper. Instead, she savored the tranquility of the courtyard, listening to the dulcet twitter of black doves nested on the palm, acacia, and olive trees. With the bench to herself, she laid down and basked in the summertime warmth, stretching her body over its length, her figure adding contours to the straight bench back, her locks of tightly coiled black hair spilling down.

"What's the matter with your brother, my child?"

Itaweret bolted upright, startled. Dedyet, mother to Itaweret and Bek and wife of the great chief of Per-Pehu, entered from the opposite side of the courtyard. A smile creased across her weath-ered, middle-aged face, her skin almost as dark as the wig of tightly curled black locks running down its sides.

Itaweret scooted aside to make room. "Oh, he's a bit upset that he lost another game of senet today. I suppose I can't blame him."

"You would act the same way if you were in his place, believe me," Dedyet said. "And while he does need to learn graciousness, your brother isn't wrong to feel the stress he does. If anything, Itaweret, I think you could stand to learn from him."

Itaweret cocked an eyebrow. "What do you mean, Mother?"

"Suffice to say, I'd think the high priestess of Mut would spend her time doing more important things than playing games with her brother. These are troubled times we're living in, after all." Itaweret's smile flopped into a frown. "Speaking of which, your father has an important guest arriving within a couple of hours, and they specifically requested your presence. You ought to put on your best for the occasion."

Itaweret wasted no time. She returned to her dressing room, washed herself clean, and slathered scented oil over her umber skin to make it glisten. She then focused on her face and hair, combing and perfuming her locks and beading their tips with gold, and lining her eyelids with black kohl. She adorned her neck and limbs with jewelry of gold, copper, and colored stones, and threw on her whitest, most translucent linen dress. Such was the work that went into making any self-respecting daughter of Kemet look presentable for public attention.

She strode out, adjusting her collar of gold, lapis-lazuli, malachite, and carnelian as she navigated through a series of painted hallways to her father's audience chamber. Who had he invited for such a formal occasion? Since he summoned her to his side, the guest was presumably a man. Men always wanted at least one young woman to decorate the scene while they talked politics, regardless of what they were discussing.

She could only pray to the gods that the mystery guest wasn't the sort who demanded anything more from women than visually appealing background decor.

She arrived in the audience chamber to find Mahu, her father—and no one else. That was a surprise. Where was the guest she'd spent hours preparing for? Only the clipping of Mahu's sandals over the tiled floor disturbed the silence within the spacious columned room as he stepped down from his great chief's throne to her. He wore his finest jewelry, whitest loincloth, and blackest braided wig, with gold rings slipped onto his long and narrow beard.

"You've come at the very best time, my child," Mahu said. His caramel-colored face seemed a shade paler than normal. "I feared you would keep our guest waiting."

"Who exactly might this man be, Father?" Itaweret asked. "He seems to have you as spooked as an antelope being stalked."

"You will see why the moment you first lay eyes on him. All I can say is that he really isn't one you want to provoke. Please conduct yourself the absolute best you can, Itaweret."

The doors at the far side of the audience chamber parted open with an echoing grind. Mahu hurried back onto his gilded throne, with Itaweret following and then standing next to him. She tilted her head up, her arms straight down, trying to look as regal as possible despite the anxious chill trickling up her spine.

A procession of men marched into the chamber, their steps loud and menacing. They were dressed in clanking panoplies of banded bronze armor, which looked like bronze pots stacked atop one another, from biggest to smallest. Such bottom-heavy suits would have invited ridicule normally, but these men wielded spears flashing reddish glints that reflected the evening sunlight. Sheathed broadswords banged along their hips as they walked.

The leader of the arriving party took off his helmet of boar-tusk platelets and shook his long mane of straight black hair. A crimson cape streamed behind him as he strutted onto the dais supporting Mahu's throne. His hazel-brown eyes scanned all around the audience chamber.

"Not unimpressive, I must say," the leader said in baritone Achaean. "It's not the most monumental pinnacle of Kemetian architecture, to be sure, but I suppose I'll have to find that in Kemet itself."

"It's the most a colonial great chief like myself could afford, I'm afraid," Mahu replied, also adopting the Achaean language for purposes of the diplomatic conversation. "Ever since the Canaanite Hyksos seized the north of Kemet and so cut us off from our mother country, we've been a bit stretched on resources."

"Such a shame. It's almost as if settling down on faraway shores wasn't so ingenious after all."

The Achaean man's gaze drifted over to Itaweret, his eyes rising and following the contours of her body. A broad grin stretched almost the full width of his olive-skinned face. "Ah, if it isn't the lovely Itaweret herself! I see the rumors do not lie. She's quite the exotic young beauty, isn't she?"

He reached a hand over to stroke Itaweret's hair. She forced herself to stand still and let him caress it, despite every impulse to back away and slap him senseless.

"Who are you, anyway?" she asked. "And what, by all the gods, do you want?"

"You haven't heard of me already? I am Scylax, king of Mycenae. And I've come to negotiate the fate of your little settlement here."

Mahu leaned forward, alarmed. "What do you mean, *our fate*? You're not plotting anything violent or destructive, are you?"

Scylax cut loose a laugh filled with hearty mockery. "My dear Mahu, you do not seem to realize how little all the Achaean people approve of your colonizing our lands. Trust me when I say that I do not speak only for myself, or even the people of Mycenae. Why, if we were to rub out the black stain that is the Kemetian presence here, every Achaean city and village would sing my praises."

He glanced up at a painted relief behind Mahu's throne, which depicted the pharaoh of Kemet holding a troop of yellow-faced men by their hair while raising a battle mace to smite them. Another row of captives knelt underneath the pharaoh's feet, ropes tightly binding their arms together. Itaweret could not shake the moment captured in the relief, nor the fact that the captives' features and attire resembled those of native Achaeans.

"After all, it's not like your colony's relations with my people have always been peaceful," Scylax continued. "Consider it a testament to my benevolence that I'm providing you with the option of survival—on two conditions."

He returned his gaze to Itaweret, who retreated a step. The disgust his eyes and words churned inside her stomach burned her with the rage of oil on fire.

"I know from your eyes exactly what one of those conditions is," she snarled.

"Itaweret!" Mahu banged his scepter on the floor of the dais. "I told you to conduct yourself the best you could. That's on behalf of all Per-Pehu."

"Your father gives sound advice, my ebony maiden," Scylax said. "Especially when I haven't even named my terms yet. The first is a regular tribute in gold and silver, which I understand you Kemetians have mined in abundance since coming here. The second, of course . . ."

The Mycenaean king thrust an arm around Itaweret's waist and pressed her against his armor, using the crushing force of his massive muscles to suppress her attempts to squirm from his hold. Only Scylax's superior strength kept her from tearing herself away and pouncing on the lustful brute to savage him with a leopardess's fury.

". . . is your daughter's hand in marriage," Scylax finished. "She'd make a fine trophy for me, wouldn't you agree?"

Mahu's eyes shifted back and forth between Itaweret and the Mycenaean king. "King Scylax, I would be willing to send you as much gold and silver as you request. Ever since we lost contact with our mother Kemet, we've little use for most of it anyway. But I am afraid we Kemetians don't normally give our daughters away to foreign rulers. It's not our custom."

"Perhaps you will think differently when you consider that I've already encamped the bulk of my army on the plain east of your city. Believe me when I say our action will be immediate if you do not honor my requests."

"Well, in that case . . . as much as I would loathe to lose my eldest child, I'd loathe even more to lose everyone else in the colony that I hold dear. My daughter, what do you think?"

Itaweret had no intention of giving anything to the despicable tyrant before her, let alone herself. Neither did she want Per-Pehu razed to the ground, and its people either massacred or forced into chains.

She thought more about it. Her father had a point. No woman wanted to lose her freedom, especially a woman with the great freedom she enjoyed, but the freedom of one woman would never outweigh the survival of an entire colony.

Nor could one man be allowed to take so many lives and wipe out an entire people because he couldn't have one woman's body.

She came upon a solution. "No man, not even a king, should feel like a woman owes him her love," she said. "If you truly desire me, O Scylax of Mycenae, you'll have to fight for it!"

Mahu banged his scepter again. "Itaweret, think about this. We haven't the strength to go to war right now."

Scylax's smile suggested he couldn't have been more amused. "On the contrary, O great chief of Per-Pehu, I look forward to it. We'll have more sport with a fair fight than merely hacking up helpless citizens anyway. Let us meet on the plain east of here."

Silence hung within the audience chamber. Finally, Mahu let out a frustrated sigh, shaking his head. "I suppose I've no longer any choice. Know only that if we win, you will have to leave our proximity empty-handed."

"And if you lose . . . well, I needn't spell that one out. Dine and sleep well tonight, my Kemetian hosts. You'll need it."

Scylax and his retainers marched out of the audience chamber, the echoes of their steps taunting the hosts until they could be heard no more.

Silence hung in the hall. Itaweret wrung her hands together while absorbing her father's harsh and incredulous expression. She felt like a child about to be blasted with a scolding lecture.

"Tell your brother about this," Mahu said. "He should know he'll be leading the defense."

Itaweret nodded and left the room.

CHAPTER TWO

When she reached the door to her brother's bedchamber, Itaweret halted, still as a stone. The sky outside shifted from red to violet, the day's heat fading into the breezy cool of night. That was not what made her shudder. Nor was it dreading her brother's reaction to Mahu's command.

Instead, she shuddered with fear for her brother's safety, for his life.

Why did Mahu pick Bek to lead Per-Pehu's garrison against the Mycenaeans? Bek had yet to see twenty summers in his whole life! Instead, she thought, their father should have announced that he would command the defense of Per-Pehu himself. True, Mahu might be well into middle age, wearing his wig to disguise the speckling of gray in his natural hair. But he was still decades away from the frailty of an old man, and still very capable of leading forces into battle and fighting himself.

Her thoughts grew angrier. What kind of man would send his adolescent son to the battlefield rather than himself? Had she misjudged her father's courage all her life?

Itaweret tapped her knuckle on Bek's door with more gentleness than usual. She didn't dare bang hard and loud. Nonetheless, a few seconds later, she heard him grumble for her to come in. "I hope you have a good explanation for everything, Sister," he said.

She creaked open the door. Bek sat on the edge of his gold-framed bed, papyrus scrolls piled on his lap as if he were a scribe hard at work. An oil lamp flickered atop one of his wooden chests, revealing more scrolls strewn all over the floor, covering the floor like a second layer of tiling.

Itaweret tiptoed around the papyrus sheets and scrolls. "You weren't lying when you said you had a lot to study," she said.

"Studying military strategy, mostly." Bek continued to read the scroll. "And considering very recent developments, that would be the best thing for me to brush upon tonight."

"You heard Father and me talking, didn't you?"

"Why not? Mother didn't say I couldn't come along to eaves-drop, did she? Regardless, I hope you're happy, Sister. Today you've sent me on a premature journey to the afterlife."

A heavy weight sank within her chest. She seated herself on the bed to comfort her brother. He nudged her away.

"Fine then!" she said, pushing him. "Would you rather I be dragged away to spend the rest of my mortal life with that savage? Besides, you should be mad at Father rather than me. He's the one who wanted you to lead the garrison!"

"Oh, so I suppose you'd prefer our father put his own life at risk for you instead? Do you think only of yourself, Itaweret? Men must die all because of one woman's foolishness!"

Any guilt or sympathy she felt for Bek's awful fate, to command a defense force against the ruthless tyrant Scylax, all but evaporated in her rage. She snatched the scroll out of his hand and ripped it in half. "If that is how you speak of your own sister, Bek, then to the twelve gates of the underworld with you! Any man . . . no, any boy who would rather sit by while the rudest barbarian ravages me could never be my brother."

She charged out of the bedchamber, her feet squishing papyrus, not bothering to step around the sheets on the floor. She slammed the door behind her.

Itaweret retreated into the darkness of the back courtyard and roared like a lioness at the star-dusted heavens. Tree branches seemed to shiver and rustle from the unspeakable blasphemies she screeched with frenzied abandon while twirling around like a tor-nado, no amount of dizziness too much to stop her. The two men she held most dear in her life had shown they did not care about her fate. Both would sooner surrender her to forced violation than receive so much as a scratch on their own hides.

Small wonder they were men; that went for the brute Scylax as well. Whether Kemetian or Achaean, men could and would never appreciate the true value of humanity's other half, the half that birthed and nursed and groomed and taught them, along with their sisters. Still, they saw themselves as the sex better fit to rule the world!

"Itaweret, are you feeling all right?" Bek's eyes twinkled with tears like her own. She never heard him approach. "I only wanted to apologize. I should not have been so blind."

"Blind to what?" she rasped, her voice hoarse from the ranting.

"Blind to your point of view. I should never have overlooked that what Scylax desired was rape. And I would do anything, even descend to the lowest cave of the underworld, before I let my dear sister suffer that very cruelty. Treat yourself to some wine, and then let's go over a plan to crush these Mycenaean savages into dust."

The rage flew out of Itaweret. Overcome by the shock of his caring, she staggered into his arms and collapsed in them. "I don't need a drink. Mut herself could not have smiled on me with greater kindness than what you did this moment, Brother." She wiped her tears away, gave herself a moment to focus, and peered into his eyes. "Now, what do you know so far about the Mycenaeans?"

Bek unrolled a papyrus scroll showing Mycenaean spearmen gathered into a rectangular formation. The front line of soldiers held cowhide shields that were each shaped like two conjoined circles. "According to my research, this is the preferred style of fighting for the Mycenaeans and the other major Achaean cities," he explained. "They call each formation a 'phalanx,' and they ram these phalanxes into each other and try to push the enemy away. Or crush them in between. If you take away the spears, it basically looks like our big shoving matches when we were kids. Only with hundreds or thousands of people."

Itaweret snickered. "Which you always complained about losing." She couldn't resist teasing him.

"Only because I was still smaller than you, Sister. Anyway, what occurred to me about these traditional Mycenaean battle tactics is that they're so direct, upfront . . . and rather sluggish. No fast maneuvers, no stealthy ambushes, nothing like that. They might have a few skirmishers and archers up front, but that's about it for range capabilities. For the most part, it's little more than two armies of men shoving each other with shields and spears."

"So, what are they going to do when someone showers them with arrows or javelins? Or strikes them at the flanks? Or, at the very least, catches them by surprise?"

Bek nodded at the question, her insight. "That there is some clever thinking. It seems I was wrong about an early journey to the afterlife. Breaking up and smiting these brutes in bronze should be easier than beating a monkey at senet."

"I can only pray so, considering your senet skills."

Bek laughed. "But you haven't seen me play against a monkey. Come back to my room tonight. Together, we will map out our strategy for vanquishing these Mycenaeans before they even know what hit them."

Itaweret heard the flutter of wings above her, the hoot of an owl. She tracked the sound to a nearby olive tree, on which the wise bird of the night had perched itself. It appeared to be a common barn owl at first glance, yet when she noticed its eyes, they seemed not to take in light but to glow, their silver-gray radiance brighter than the moon itself.

"What is with that owl's eyes?" Itaweret asked.

Bek squinted toward the tree as she pointed. "Where? I don't see the eyes . . . or the owl."

She blinked. The owl and its strange silver-gray eyes had vanished without a sound, flying away in stealthy silence. Had it been an illusion? Or had a new type of owl found Per-Pehu to its liking?

Kleno sat on a log within a small patch of woodland. The surrounding oak and olive trees muffled the noises of soldiers' banter, laughter, and gluttony coming from her brother's encampment to the east. They also shaded her from the Kemetian colony that rose beyond the western plain. The hooded wolf-skin cloak over her tunic granted her warmth in the night and hid her face with its sprawling shadow.

The flapping of wings announced Athena's return. Kleno held a gloved hand out to welcome the silver-eyed owl, which landed on her finger, its talons gripping firmly. She stroked the feathers on the bird's head as if it were a pet cat.

"O gray-eyed Athena, what news do you bring?" she asked.

"I know what the Kemetians are planning for the battle, my priestess."To an ordinary mortal, the owl's reply sounded like unintelligible hooting. However, Kleno and her trained ears heard the voice of a goddess. "They want to ambush your brother's men from the cover of the trees on the battlefield."

"Thank you, O wise one." Kleno rewarded the owl with a dead rat from her satchel. "My brother will love to hear this."

Kleno stood and walked out of the wood, Athena perched on her fingers. She re-entered the camp of leather tents to find the Mycenaean soldiers huddling around campfires, gorging themselves on meat and bread they had plundered from the countryside. Enslaved men and women from other Achaean cities entertained them with lyres and flutes.

On a stool outside the massive center tent brooded King Scylax. "Had enough peace and quiet for the night, big sister?" he asked.

"No, but I bring back something you would appreciate even more. Athena has told me how the Kemetians plan to beat you."

Scylax leaned toward her. "Tell me everything."

CHAPTER THREE

The earliest shafts of sunlight rose from behind a line of rugged peaks above the eastern horizon. Underneath a sky dotted with pink-bottomed clouds, a plain of yellowed grass stretched between the foothills and Per-Pehu's mudbrick ramparts. Scattered over the otherwise open expanse were copses of cypress, olive, and date palm trees fenced in by thick scrubby bushes.

Within one of these patches of woodland, Bek and a platoon of his most trained warriors lay under the cool and shaded cover of the trees. The spots of green paint on their skin, mixed in with stripes as yellow as the grass, further blended them into their surroundings. No one uttered a single word, not even in whispers. Only the morning birds sang.

Bek had spent the better half of the past night dispersing the colony's garrison among the clusters of trees and shrubs, but he felt not the least bit groggy. The battle to save his sister, and possibly the entire colony, would take place on this morning. The excitement and anticipation had sparked more than enough restless energy. The soft gleam of the copper bulb topping his battle mace provided even more inspiration.

The morning quiet ended with the hoot of an owl flying overhead. The bird glimpsed quickly down with its silver-gray eyes before it disappeared. Bek recalled that Itaweret had seen an owl like that the night before, with something strange about it. Was there something to that, or did the swelling tension prompt his eyes into deceiving him?

Something whooshed and landed with a wet, piercing noise. One of the men nearby screamed and croaked a death rattle. Bek looked over. Sticking out of the poor youth's back was a bronze-pointed javelin.

A barbarous ululating cry rose from the far side of the grove. Leaping out of the vegetation behind the Kemetians, olive-skinned men in brief red skirts hurled missiles like the javelin Bek had just seen. Despite their lack of body armor, these skirmishers wore the boar-tusk helmets of the Mycenaean soldiers who had marched beside Scylax.

It couldn't be! How were they here? Bek's calculated ambush had been foiled by one Scylax had set up.

Bek's men fell to his left and right, either from javelins or the slashing knives the skirmishers used whenever they got within an arm's reach of the defenders. With the advantage of surprise falling firmly into Mycenaean hands, the defenders had no chance to strike back. All they could do was leave their cover and flee into the open.

After blowing his copper bugle, Bek and his troops burst out of the trees into the open field. Meeting them there was the rest of the Kemetian garrison, also flushed out of their hiding positions. The Kemetians were herded into a jumbled mass in the middle of the plain, the Mycenaean javelin-men still harrying and eating away at the defenders' flanks with their remaining ammunition.

"Shields outward!" Bek yelled. "Form a shell!" The Kemetians covered their sides and heads with a turtle-like shell of cowhide shields. The javelins kept raining upon them, but instead of sickening death cries from their own, Bek and his troops heard harmless thunks. He thanked Sekhmet, the lioness-masked goddess of war, for this protective respite.

Finally, the downpour of javelins stopped. Bek breathed heavily with relief—but not for long. Upon he and his man came the clanking of bronze, the beating of sandaled feet on the grass, and warlike hooting in Achaean.

It was Scylax's phalanx.

They arrived in bronze, equipped with spears and double-domed shields. Unlike the organized illustrations in Bek's scrolls, they did not advance as a rectangle. Instead, their foremost ranks spread out to the left and right to form a concave line, like a bow being shoved back into the body, enveloping his troops like the jaws of a crocodile before chomping down onto a fish. If they tried to weather another attack, Bek realized, they would be crushed between the two prongs of the Mycenaean phalanx. But they couldn't run, either. That would be viewed as cowardice, costing them the lives of the whole colony—not to mention Itaweret's freedom.

The only way out was *toward* the enemy, right into the center of their formation.

Bek brandished his mace with a bloodthirsty roar. "Men of Per-Pehu, charge!"

Like a gigantic rhinoceros of men, shields, and weaponry, the defenders sprinted with explosive speed and crashed into the heart of the Mycenaean phalanx, chanting the battle songs of Kemet as they ran. Their spears stabbed and punctured, axes slashed and cleaved, and clubs dented bronze armor and crushed bone within underlying flesh. Blood and spilled organs sprayed everywhere, paving the ground slick and polluting the air with the stench of death.

It was not the first time in his young life Bek had taken lives. He and his father had cultivated a fondness for hunting in the countryside outside Dedenu, whether they pursued fowl, wild boar, deer, or larger animals that threatened the farmers' crops. Never on those hunts had he brought down a creature with the same fury that flamed in his soul as he hammered away at the Mycenaeans with his mace. Never had he relished the spilling of blood and cracking of skulls as he did now.

After all, these invaders were not mere animals doing what animals did naturally, without free will. They were human beings with the power of choice. They had chosen to pledge their loyalty to a savage brute. If any creatures in the world *deserved* to be killed, these barbarians did. Not even their ridiculous panoplies could save them from his vengeful wrath.

A bronze spearhead pierced through the flat cowhide of Bek's shield. It came from Scylax, the king of Mycenae himself. With one wrench of his arm, he forced the shield out of Bek's grasp.

"So, you're the son of Mahu?" Scylax asked sarcastically, cackling with every word. "He couldn't be bothered to fight me himself, could he? No matter. The tide of battle shall turn again to my favor when I'm finished with you, boy!"

Scylax thrust again. A sharp pain cut across the side of Bek's torso. Though twirling from the blow like a dust-devil, Bek smashed his mace through the shaft of the Mycenaean's spear, splintering it in half. He drew back for another swing until Scylax rammed him with his shield, knocking him back onto the gore-swamped grass.

Bek threw his broken spear aside and tore out his sword. He rolled over the ground to avoid the Mycenaean warrior-king's stabs until his adversary stepped onto his torso and pinned him down. Scylax sneered with demonic glee as he prepared his killing blow.

It did not come. Another Kemetian swung his ax, the blow landing's close to Scylax's head. When the Mycenaean tyrant withdrew to do away with his new attacker, Bek sprung up and delivered a glancing blow across the back of his helmet. The stunned Scylax stumbled until he toppled onto his knees.

"Not so tough, are you, O king of Mycenae?" Bek taunted.

He prepared his own death blow: thrusting the mace straight through his arch-enemy's skull. Before it hit the mark, Scylax parried the blow with his sword, chopping the mace into two.

Now Bek was disarmed. He carried no weapon that could parry Scylax's sword, not even the puny dagger that hung from his belt. No longer did he have hope of slaying the barbarian warlord. He quickly looked around to see that his men had been whittled down to a paltry minority sprinkled between the Mycenaean fighters. Even if Scylax were to fall, his remaining army could still butcher the entire Kemetian garrison into extinction. Time to escape.

Bek blew a high-pitched shriek through his bugle, then commanded his remaining troops to run westward. He and his army had transformed from leopards waiting in ambush, and then a herd of bold, charging rhinoceroses, into a decimated flock of gazelles leaping away from the triumphant jeers and roars of the Mycenaeans.

Bek, son of Mahu, and heir to the throne of great chief of Per-Pehu, had failed his people. He'd underestimated his enemy.

But something didn't add up, he thought as he and his men ran clear of the Mycenaeans. How had Scylax and his skirmishers figured out his strategy? How had they found him and his men? If the attackers had not driven his garrison out of hiding, he might have defeated Scylax's phalanx with the element of surprise. There had to be some explanation, even if only the gods knew it.

If anyone Bek knew could divine the answer, it would be his sister Itaweret, high priestess of Mut.

CHAPTER FOUR

The idol of the goddess Mut stood twice the height of a human being, safely tucked within the temple's sanctuary chamber. Her black diorite skin and the gold paint covering her pleated dress and jewelry shone from the braziers burning on the dais at her feet, as did the tall copper scepter she clutched. The firelight danced to the rumble of drums, the twanging of harps, and the rattling of *sistra* of the temple musicians while a chorus of priestesses sang their prayers to the goddess.

Before the limestone platform on which the sculpture stood, Itaweret knelt while joining the other priestesses in their songs. She spent the entire dawn leading the ritual in the sanctuary, hoping that the goddess would hear her prayers and grant divine blessing upon the men fighting to defend the colony. Mut would empower Bek and his men, protect them from as much harm as possible, or wreak havoc on Scylax and his Mycenaean attackers. It did not matter which if it helped the people of Per-Pehu in the end.

"Itaweret! Sister!"

Bek's voice rang from outside the sanctum. He ran into the room and collapsed onto the floor, spatters of blood mottling his skin and loincloth. "We . . . lost."

Sheer horror choked Itaweret speechless. The singing stopped. She pulled up her brother and embraced him fully. She thanked the mercy of fate for letting her brother survive, even if he brought only the most horrible news.

"I . . . don't know how, but Scylax figured out . . . our strategy," Bek said, panting heavily. "He flushed us out of hiding and then . . . crushed us like a herd of elephants. He and his men . . . will be breaking through our doors any moment now."

"This cannot be!" Itaweret turned to the idol of Mut. "O mighty Mut, how could you let this happen?"

A thunderous boom reverberated within the temple's halls of columns, seeming to rattle the reliefs and hieroglyphs inscribed on them. Soon after, a flash of golden light flooded Itaweret's vision, retaining its brilliance even when she shut her eyes.

The eyes of Mut's idol shone like the blinding brilliance of the sun itself, dispelling all shadow within her sanctum. "I have heard your prayers, my dear high priestess." A resonant female voice spoke, every syllable pulsing within Itaweret's head. "It is I, Mut, consort of the Sun and Creator Amun-Ra. Trust me when I say I would have done everything I could to help you and your people in this time of need. Alas, I fear there is another goddess out there working to undermine my influence even as I speak to you."

"Another goddess? Who might that be?" Itaweret asked.

"Neither you nor any of the other children of Kemet know of her, yet she is no less real than I or my brethren. I speak of the Achaean Athena, daughter of Zeus of Olympus. Through her priestess Kleno, sister of Scylax, it is she who thwarted your brother on the battlefield."

"How?"

"She sent a spy . . . through the air."

"Then what must we do?" Bek asked. "We can't let that barbarian lay a hand on my sister, or anyone else in Per-Pehu!"

"The solution is simple, but it will be difficult," the goddess replied. "You must eliminate Scylax as king of Mycenae. Not only your own people, but the Achaean people as well, will thank you for it. You and your sister must leave this colony for the north and east. In the first village you see on the other side of the mountains, you will find your answer. One more thing before you go . . ."

The glow from the goddess's eyes drifted away and fell onto the copper scepter. It rose out of her grip with a shrill scrape and floated toward Itaweret until it dropped at her feet.

"Take this scepter with you, my child," Mut said. "It will protect you against any enemy you confront. Be it man, beast, or demon. Now both of you, go."

The light faded from the scepter when Itaweret picked it up. She and Bek had sparred throughout their whole lives, but that was little more than children's play. Never had she anticipated that she would have need for a weapon in real life.

"Surely Bek and I can't go all by ourselves?" Itaweret pleaded.

The light returned to the goddess's eyes. "Fear not, for you will not be alone. I will be with you, always . . ." Her parting words echoed for a minute within the sanctum.

A second later, stone blocks began to grind against one another. Itaweret hopped back as the line of floor tiles sank into a succession of steps between the idol's supporting dais and where she stood, leading down into what appeared to be a subterranean hatch.

Of course. A secret passageway out of the temple. She should have known. Either that, or Mut just created an escape for them out of nothing.

Bek hauled up one of the temple's braziers. "We could use some lighting down there."

Itaweret looked toward the other priestesses. She wanted to invite them on the journey, but she had no provisions, no time to stock up. Leaving them behind to fend for themselves against Scylax and his barbarians when barged into the city would be cruel, to be sure, but she saw no better solution.

She looked into the eyes of each priestess, certain she was seeing them for the last time. "May the goddess watch over every one of you as well," she said.

Itaweret hugged the copper scepter of Mut and followed her brother down the steps into darkness.

The cedar gate to Per-Pehu opened for Scylax and his army with a slow, solemn groan. While standing behind their battlements atop the gatehouse, the city guards shot down glares of resentment at the Mycenaeans like arrows as they passed through. Many held their bows, quivers, and spears close to their bodies, ready to wield them in defense of their home. A futile, final defense.

Not that Scylax minded the guards on the wall. He had already won the battle. What little remained of Per-Pehu's pitiful military could be crushed into the mud with little effort.

Trumpets announced the Mycenaeans' victory parade down the city's main avenue. They may have been splattered with blood and organs, but Scylax and his men marched with the disciplined confidence of triumphant conquerors. They largely ignored the dark-skinned masses of Kemetian citizens watching from the flat-roofed houses and alleyways alongside the avenue, hissing curses and wailing lamentations when they weren't chucking stones and shards of broken pottery at the soldiers. Scylax found the Kemetians' childish protests amusing, especially since everything they hurled harmlessly bounced off their armor.

Scylax arrived at the entrance to the colonial palace. It was already open for him. He strutted toward the complex's audience hall, passing rows of granite statues portraying the colony's former great chiefs. When he was done dealing with Mahu, he would break off all their faces, beheading the full line of leaders, even if they were now only statues.

Scylax entered the audience hall to find Mahu waiting on his throne. The Kemetian great chief sat with a resigned composure that, Scylax thought, seemed far too relaxed for a man about to lose what he cared about the most.

"Well, well, it looks like I've won your little war, Lord Mahu," Scylax said. "You know the terms of our arrangement. I beat your son in battle, and you provide the tribute—and your daughter—to me."

Mahu smiled, a look far more defiant than nervous. "I know not where my daughter is now, but she isn't here. You can have as much gold as you desire, King Scylax." He paused for a long moment. "But you'll never have her."

Scylax's cheeks flared, as red as the bloodstains on his armor. He stomped over to Mahu and clenched a hand tight around his throat, lifting him off his throne. "You cheat! How could you betray me like that?"

"Did you honestly think I'd sell my beloved daughter away to be used by an overgrown jackal like you?" Mahu croaked.

"I did expect you to have enough sense of self-preservation—not to mention the preservation of all your people—to honor all terms of our agreement." Scylax grabbed his sword with his free hand and pressed the tip into the bottom of Mahu's jaw, pricking the skin and drawing a trickle of blood. "I see I was in error."

Footsteps in the chamber distracted him. Scylax looked to the side, in their direction. A Kemetian woman of middle years entered from a side doorway. She wasn't that unattractive, he mused, even if not as youthful as Itaweret.

"Let my husband go!" The woman pointed a finger like a spear.

"Dedyet, stay out of this!" Mahu cried, his voice little more than a gurgle against the pressure Scylax clamped onto his throat.

"Ah, I see you have a bride of your own," Scylax said. "The girl's mother. A bit more weathered than I prefer, but I suppose I'll take her as a temporary substitute."

"If you dare lay your filthy hands on my wife—"

Scylax thrust his sword through Mahu's skull's, taking the great chief of Per-Pehu out of his misery. And out of the world. He tossed the Kemetian ruler's body onto the dais like a sack of grain fresh off the boat.

"You monster!"

As she screamed, Dedyet whipped out a slender bronze dagger and jumped with shrieking rage at Scylax. He escaped her with a simple sidestep and parried her weapon with a swipe of his own, disarming her with the blow. He flung his arm around her waist and pinned her against his breastplate. "Perhaps you will not be my wife. But you should make a fine slave for my house if you cooperate!"

Dedyet pounded her fists against Scylax, squirming with the fury of a lashing python. She stopped only when he washed his sword with blood again, the blood that spilled from her back and spine. She landed right next to her husband, together in death as in life, at once beautiful and pathetic.

Scylax heard another woman's breathing. He turned quickly, on highest alert for any other surprise visitors. It was Kleno, who appeared with Athena on her finger. "I know where Itaweret and her brother went," Kleno said. "Athena tells me they headed north and east, toward the mountains."

"Then follow them before they get too far away," Scylax replied. "I'll send some of my best warriors with you. As for the rest of the army . . . by all the gods, will we have fun with this city tonight!"

He threw back his head and let out his heartiest laugh, his latest kills at his feet, already dreaming of the plunder and slaves that awaited him and his men.

CHAPTER FIVE

No torches burned inside the tunnel beneath the temple of Mut. Only the brazier Bek carried behind her drove back the blackness, and it was dimming with every passing second. Itaweret occasionally paused to search the floor for branches that she could toss into the brazier, but found nothing but cold and damp stone.

Finally, they reached a rectangular outline of light at the tunnel's end. By the mercy of fate, the pair had not stumbled into any booby-traps, nor run into any dead ends branching off from the main passage. While dark, the journey was not as perilous as Itaweret had feared . . .

Hopefully, it would stay that way.

"How do you know this doesn't lead to a trap?" Bek asked.

"Think about it. Why would Mut lead us into a trap? Don't you trust her enough, Brother?"

"Assuming that was Mut speaking to us. What if it was that Achaean demon she talked about, that Athena?"

Itaweret fought hard within herself to ignore him and the possibility he raised. It was a valid point, if she were honest with herself, but it seemed unlikely that an Achaean deity like Athena could penetrate the sanctum of Mut. At least she hoped so. And hope was all they had left.

Itaweret walked up to the rectangle of light and pressed her shoulder against the surface, feeling the same cool stone texture as the tunnel's walls. She pushed all her strength onto the door, groaning from exertion and the exhausting day, until it fell forward with a hard thud and crumbled outside.

A flood of daylight blinded her. Once her eyes readjusted from the subterranean darkness, she found herself on the summit of a grassy hill that sloped into a gravelly beach beside the sea. The set-ting sun gilded the crests of the waves, but the colors of the sky graded ominously, from dark red to black. Itaweret wrinkled her nose from the smell of smoke and burnt flesh.

Behind the hill, the city in which she had lived her entire life bloomed into a colossal inferno of flame. The fires that roared on rooftops, together with thick black rivers of smoke, obscured any sight of the carnage that, she realized, must have clogged and already begun to rot over the streets. Still, she could make out a stream of people being herded out through the city gate, prodded along by Mycenaeans in their bronze suits.

They were her fellow citizens of Per-Pehu. Her people, friends and neighbors, reduced to human livestock in one evening.

"How dare they!" Bek shook his fist while watching what she watched, quaking with rage. "We've got to do something!"

"We will, Brother. We wouldn't be out here if we weren't going to do something about it. But we cannot fight now. Come on!"

She took his hand. They descended the hill to a dirt path that meandered northeastward. The cover of the olive and cypress trees alongside it, together with shadows that grew darker with each pass-ing minute, would conceal them from any prowling Mycenaeans.

She hoped.

Less than two hours later, the scarlet heavens faded into blackness almost as pure as that within the tunnel. Now their only light was the half-moon and dusting of tiny stars around it, giving off a faint white glow reflected upon the vegetation and stones. Itaweret hud-dled close to Bek as they hiked up the path through the foothills, pausing only to pick up sticks to feed the fire in the brazier. If there was one thing to praise the wilderness for, it was an abundance of cheap firewood.

They ascended higher into the hills, climbing until the open, scrubby landscape of the low plains gave way to oak and pine for-ests that girdled the mountains. They climbed over fallen logs and boulders strewn about with increasing density. If walking uphill had not already worn away at the strength in their legs, maneu-vering around these obstacles in the terrain taxed their muscles to aching even more.

Underneath the soft fragrance of the pines, Itaweret's nostrils flared, capturing another odor, more rancid and unpleasant. She traced the scent to the gleaming, red-spattered bones of a lamb, flies buzzing around the few scraps of meat that clung to it. She had seen cattle and goats sacrificed to the gods in the temple complex at Per-Pehu, but never witnessed their gory remains in a state like this. The sight almost shoved her last meal from her stomach into her throat.

"How could this have died?" she asked.

Bek crouched over the bones and ran his finger over one of five parallel scars raked across the ribcage. He pointed to a weathered impression in the nearby earth, broader than a human hand, with claw marks sticking out before each of its five toes.

"I would have guessed a lion, but cats in general don't leave prints like this," Bek said. "Normally they retract their claws, so they wouldn't show like they do here."

"Could it be a dog?" Itaweret asked. "Or a jackal? Or one of those gray monsters the Achaeans call wolves?"

Bek shook his head. "Much, much too big for any of those. Truth be told, I have no idea. It must be a kind of monster we've never seen in our lives."

Back home, everyone inside Per-Pehu's walls had heard travelers' stories of the beasts that roamed the wilds beyond the colony. Some spoke of cannibalistic men with singular eyes or the heads of bulls, giant swamp-dwelling serpents, or fire-breathing creatures that were part goat, part lion, and part snake. Itaweret had always considered the descriptions too ridiculous to be real. More frightening were the accounts of hulking beasts with dog-like faces and claws like knives, giant cats with dagger-long fangs, and ill-tempered elephants covered in shaggy hair. Those stories sounded almost truthful.

Itaweret wrung her hands around Mut's scepter, shivering with a dread colder than the nocturnal air itself. "Do you know whether it could be nearby?" she asked.

"I don't know," Bek said. "The tracks are a little worn. It could have left here hours or even a day ago."

Two glowing specks of yellow blinked behind a nearby patch of bushes. Leaves rustled and branches snapped as the specks drifted toward them. The furry outline of a thick, stocky body gleamed from the brazier's firelight. The creature's snout was long like a dog's, but its ears were smaller and more rounded. As it panted and grunted, it exuded the same stink of decayed flesh as the sheep carcass.

Itaweret took a step back from the lumbering animal. "What do they call things like that?"

"A bear, I believe," Bek whispered. "Stand your ground. That could scare him off."

Itaweret forced herself to stay put and waved the scepter of Mut like a warrior's staff as Bek shook the brazier back and forth at the beast. Rearing ten feet into the air on its hind feet, the bear curled its lips back, exposing pointed canines. It uncorked a menacing roar while brandishing clawed forepaws.

With a single swat, the bear knocked Itaweret's scepter out of her hands. She jumped to grab it, but the bear seized the scepter in its mouth and tossed it into the darkness. It swiped at her bosom, raking through the linen cloth and her skin with its claws. Sudden pain swept through her chest as she collapsed to the ground.

Bek thrust his brazier again, the heated ash landing on the bear's backside. Now aggravated, the bear turned away from Itaweret, roared, and charged him. The bear's attack on Bek gave her enough time to crawl over and retrieve her scepter. Just as the bear was about to punch the brazier out of Bek's grasp, she chucked the scepter into its shoulder.

Her blow distracted the beast for another second. Then it swung around and barreled toward her again. She had no other weapon to beat it aside.

Another roar followed.

All the children of Kemet could recognize that deep feline roar. Along with it appeared a pair of yellow eyes, set in a bright tawny form. The big cat sprang from the blackness and landed on the bear. The two creatures rolled in the dirt in a chaotic melee of biting and slashing.

The battle ended with the crackle of bone. The bear fell limp, a river of blood gushing from its neck, and more blood spilling from slashing cuts all over its body. The bear's slayer stood over it, roaring with a savage exultation.

Itaweret and Bek looked upon the largest lion they had ever seen, one with a thick dark mane and faint leopard-like spots on its flanks. She had heard stories of giant spotted lions roaming the countries north of the Great Green Sea, but according to those same stories, they'd died out. Was this the very last, or did it have a whole pride behind it? If the latter, would they be seeking dinner?

Itaweret could only hope the bear's big and meaty carcass would take the lion's mind off her and Bek.

Then, a voice, a proud voice in the Achaean language: "That's a good boy, Xiphos!"

A young Achaean man in a sleeveless wool tunic walked toward them, carrying a wooden shepherd's staff. He stroked the big cat's mane as if it were a tame dog while it gorged itself on the dead bear. Much to Itaweret's surprise, the lion tolerated the boy's touch, rather than fending him off like any truly wild animal.

Itaweret brushed droplets of blood off her clothing and jewelry. "Xiphos? Is he your pet or something?"

"My father brought him in when he was a cub," the Achaean youth said. "No need to fear him, my lady. He's as gentle as a puppy *unless* you provoke him. Are you folks all right? It's not every day we have black people come to these parts…even less so those that can speak our tongue."

"Why do you call us 'black' people?" Bek asked. "Our people are various shades of brown, some of us darker than others. If we are 'black,' would that make you, what, 'white'?"

The Achaean chuckled. "No use arguing over what we call each other. Trust me, I've heard far nastier names for your kind of people. Name's Philos. And you two?"

Itaweret did not want to know those "nastier" names. "I am Itaweret, high priestess of Mut from Per-Pehu. And this is my brother, Bek, son of the Great Chief Mahu."

"Aye, so you're from the colony over the hills." Philos looked up and down Itaweret's body, his eyes following her contours in much the same gazing way as Scylax of Mycenae. "And, by Aphrodite, are you fine to look at, scratches and all! Nice curves, especially."

Itaweret shook her head and grumbled. Achaean or Kemetian, white or black, men were all the same. Though she had to admit, the muscular young Achaean, with his long flowing black hair, wasn't a wholly unattractive specimen.

"Anyway, either of you wouldn't have seen a little ewe around these parts, would you?" Philos asked.

"We saw a sheep's *skeleton*," Bek replied. "We think the bear ate it sometime back."

"Hades be damned, then! Xiphos and I have been looking for her the past couple of days. At least she was only one ewe. So, what are you two Kemetians doing out here?"

"In case you haven't heard, Per-Pehu has been brutally sacked by King Scylax of Mycenae," Itaweret said. "Our goddess Mut has sent us a quest northeast, one that will lead to Scylax's defeat. We hope it does, anyway. She told us that we would find our answer in the first village over the mountains."

Philos scratched his hair. "By Zeus, that's *my* village! I don't know why we'd know how to beat the king of Mycenae, out of all people in the world. But, if your goddess says so, I ought to help you the best I can."

"How far is your village, anyway?"

"A few more hills to the east. But we ought to rest here for the night. Xiphos doesn't like being dragged away from his meals, and I think we're all damned tired anyway."

Bek yawned. "Yeah, tell me about it."

Itaweret nodded. Almost every muscle burned from straining, even beyond her wounds from the bear's attack. Her stomach groaned with hunger. Once the lion filled himself, she wouldn't mind cooking leftovers of the bear over a fire lit by Bek's brazier. Never had she eaten bear meat, but food was food in uncivilized places.

She looked up at the tree line and caught the flicker of little eyes. They weren't the yellow eyes of a bear, lion, or other predator, but silver-gray eyes . . . familiar eyes.

She blinked. The eyes were gone.

CHAPTER SIX

Philos cracked his eyelids open and noticed the brazier had burned itself empty. Not even the tiniest wisp of smoke rose from it, although a faint burning scent still lingered along with the mustiness of the forest floor and the rotting stench that the dead bear had begun to exude.

The light of sunrise beamed through the treetops' screen of leaves and pine needles. The golden rays fell on his skin, its pleasant warmth massaging away the last of the night's damp chill. With a relaxed moan, he raised himself up from the log he'd used for a bed and brushed the splinters out of his hair.

On the other side of the makeshift campsite, the two Kemetians were still in deep sleep, resting their heads on rocks as if they were pillows. The tight coils of their dark hair were the only cushions for their heads over such hard surfaces, Philos thought. Regardless of how strange they appeared, he could not turn his eyes away from them. Especially the woman. If anything, Itaweret's glossy dark complexion bestowed a unique allure, like a rare gemstone mined from the distant south. So too did her full and luscious lips, her rounded facial features, and the exquisite foreign jewelry bedecking her figure. Not to mention her wide hips and the ample backside behind them.

The Kemetian woman opened her dark eyes. "Why do you keep looking at me like that, Achaean boy?"

Philos recoiled until he fell over the log. "Um, I was only curious. Like I said last night, we don't get your kind here often."

"Curious, really? I would've thought you had something . . . more in mind?"

"I did say you were fine to look at, didn't I? Unusually so, in fact. Let me put it this way, I don't see a girl like you every day. And, honestly, I rather like—"

"So, you think I look exotic?" Itaweret chided. "I suppose a woman of Kemet like myself would be, from your point of view. Our peoples do look . . . different, after all."

Philos responded with a sheepish laugh. "Well, 'exotic' is in the eye of the beholder. It shouldn't be a bad thing, anyway. Right?"

Bek jerked up and interposed himself in front of Itaweret. "Hold up there, Achaean! You're not trying to get with my sister, are you?"

"Why not?" Philos said, looking down at his own lighter skin. "Do you have a problem with, ah, people of different colors getting together?"

Itaweret sighed. "Look, Philos, you *are* somewhat handsome for your race, even if you do come on a *little* strong. But you Achaeans are still barbarians, after all, and Bek and I have lost our entire home—and possibly our whole family—to your kind of people."

Philos's face flared with the heat of anger. "No, not *my* people. It was those warmongering Mycenaeans, not Achaeans from *my* little village. Unlike you Kemetians, we Achaeans don't all follow the same king or obey the same rules!"

"True, you instead prefer to squabble with one another when you're not threatening our colony," Bek said. "Like true savages. I for one wouldn't trust someone from such a quarrelsome people with my big sister."

"Then fine!" Philos stood up and grabbed his crook. "If you can't trust even one Achaean, there's no point in me helping you. Either fend for yourself out here or go back to Kemet whence your people came! Come on, Xiphos, let's head home without these two ingrates."

The lion, who had been sleeping on top of his kill, replied with a whimpering moan.

"Bek and I can't simply go back to Kemet," Itaweret said. "Not while the Mycenaeans have carried off the rest of our people. We can't let them suffer any longer."

With a shake of his head, Philos sighed. "Look, let's make a deal. I take you to my village, where you find what you're looking for, and you treat me with as much respect as you would a fellow Kemetian. I won't ask for anything more."

Itaweret batted her eyelashes while flashing a mocking smirk. "Not even my love and adoration?"

Philos snorted. "Not even that . . . yet. Now, we best be off. Odds are, Scylax and his minions could be looking for you. I wouldn't idle around if I were you."

He whistled to Xiphos, who hopped off the bear carcass and let his master caress his mane. From the corner of his eye, he sneaked one more glance at Itaweret and sighed. If they were going to be stuck with one another for at least two more days, Philos thought, the Kemetian girl and her brother would need to shed their prejudice and learn to trust him. He would do everything he could to earn that. Maybe then, if the fates were kind enough, Itaweret would come to feel the same way about him that he did toward her.

If so, a girl would like him. For once in his life.

May the goddess watch over every one of you as well.

Sennuwy would never forget the final words the High Priestess Itaweret said to her and the rest of Mut's clergy before leaving their temple with her brother. Not a minute had gone by when Sennuwy did not hear them in her head, repeating over and over. Not a minute over the past several days.

If only she could keep her faith in those words. Itaweret had spoken them with the fullest sincerity, like everything else she said. That Sennuwy could never doubt. Yet, after witnessing their city being sacked, and spending every moment since yoked and wristbound to a human chain of her surviving countrymen and women, she doubted whether any of the gods still watched over them.

The only time when Sennuwy and the rest of Per-Pehu's remaining citizens enjoyed any respite from the wooden yokes on their necks came when the Mycenaean army stopped to camp. The captive Kemetians were crammed into a makeshift corral with a few soldiers appointed to guard them. Otherwise, they wore yokes and ropes, marching without break over rugged terrain, their long line trailing the army and its baggage train. The only food and water they received were scraps the Mycenaean horsemen were willing to offer as they rode alongside.

Whether in yoke or corral, Sennuwy could never escape the barbarians' eyes. She could not even whisper to the other captives, lest any of the guards think she was arranging a scheme to break free and punish her with a sharp lash of the whip.

Instead, she would sing. That would take her people's minds off the exhausting drudgery of the walk. Even the guards might appreciate the music, although she did not know whether they could understand a word she sang.

She sang of the glory of Kemet and Per-Pehu's past, of the wealth collected through trade and the excavation of gold and silver. She sang of the terrible crimes the Achaean barbarians of Mycenae inflicted upon the colony's people, how they tore down its grandeur in their lust for plunder while slaughtering the men and raping the women. She sang of how the city was reduced to mounds of smoking rubble, how broken weapons and mutilated corpses clogged its streets, and how the survivors were dragged away from their homes and forced into the yokes. And she sang prayers for the gods of Kemet to come down, break away her people's chains and lead them to rebuild what had been destroyed.

Sennuwy did not sing alone. The woman shuffling in front of her answered her lyrics by chanting her own, as did the man behind her. The singing spread back and forth along the chain of captives until all the people of Per-Pehu sang together, stamping their feet in rhythm like drumbeats.

CHAPTER SEVEN

Twice **the sun sailed westward over the pine-robed mountains,** until the path descended into a broad, flat valley bisected by a slender stream. At the point where the forest stopped and the open scrub of the valley floor began, a denuded tree trunk rose with the sun-bleached skull of a bull mounted on top. Dangling on leather straps like chimes from the bovine horns were more skulls . . . human skulls.

Itaweret's hands turned cold and wet on her scepter as she examined the macabre display. "You sure you've brought us the right way, Philos?"

The Achaean shepherd slapped her shoulder with a laugh. "Oh, that's only there to scare enemies and unwelcome intruders away."

Bek rolled his eyes. "Very funny."

"Regardless, you two should be happy. We're here at last. And you can thank Xiphos and me for that." Philos gave his lion another pat on the mane.

Itaweret shrugged. "Your pet is good at keeping the wolves and bears away, I'll give you that."

The humid shade beneath the trees faded into dry warmth as they glided across the valley to the stream's bank. They stopped for rest. After two days trekking through the cool of the wooded highlands, Itaweret never expected she would welcome the heat that cooked the Achaean plains. As she treated herself to the trickling water, splashing it over her brow and drinking from cupped hands, she heard something far away . . . the lowing of cattle? The bleating of sheep? The wind carried a subtle whiff of their dung.

"Philos! Your father's been worried sick about you!"

A short and stocky Achaean in a simple, dirt-stained tunic ran out from the reedy growth beside the stream and grabbed Philos by the shoulder. The skin of the stranger's bearded face was almost as dark red as copper.

"Gelon!" Philos gave the bearded man a tight hug. "You need not worry, I'm safe. Unfortunately, the same couldn't be said of the ewe—it appears a bear got her. Oh, and I've brought a couple of guests."

Gelon turned to face Itaweret and Bek, squinting while his lips curled back in apparent disgust. "You mean these two *melanchroes* strangers?"

Itaweret had never heard that strange phrase, but she could tell from the man's tone that it wasn't complimentary. "What do you mean, '*melanchroides*'?"

"Trust me, you *don't* want to know," Philos said. "Gelon, shame on you for your inhospitality. These are Itaweret and Bek, Kemetian refugees from Per-Pehu. I beg you, please treat them as you would a fellow Achaean."

"But they aren't fellow Achaeans," Gelon growled. "The Kemetians have been making war on us, stealing from us, and raping our womenfolk ever since they showed up on our land. Why, they took my mother away and killed my father! Why should any of us trust those melanchroides?"

Bek drew his dagger. "If you say that cursed word one more time, you *will* pay for it, Achaean jackal!"

"Very well, then, *mauros*."

"Oh, for the love of Aphrodite, stop it!" Philos smacked Gelon on the head with the tip of his crook. "Itaweret and Bek, I'm sorry for my old friend's behavior. I never would have thought him so small-minded."

"Then you need better judgment when making friends," Bek grumbled.

"Enough of this!" Itaweret said. "Philos and Gelon, please lead us to your village."

Gelon spat out something vulgar in protest, but he shut his mouth when Philos gave him a stern look. Even Xiphos seemed to growl at his master's supposed friend—not that Itaweret had any idea what the shepherd saw in the rude barbarian that brought them together as friends in the first place. Whatever it was, the exchange whittled away much of her desire to reach the village. What if such attitudes were normal for Philos's neighbors? What would she have to put up with next?

Narrowing her eyes to filter out the blinding brightness of the sun, Itaweret looked up to the sky and called upon the goddess Mut in a whisper. "I sure hope you know what you're doing."

Itaweret and Bek followed the Achaeans along the stream as it broadened into a slower-flowing river, its banks shaded by olive and palm trees. The narrow forests gave way to miniature tracts of tilled earth, with tufts of young wheat and barley plants sprouting between the grooves. Crude wooden fences divided the small plots of cropland from one another, the fences wearing wide-leafed grapevines as if they were lush festoons.

"The growing season's started early this year," Philos said. "Demeter be praised."

The sight of farmland lining the riverbank reminded Itaweret of what she had been told about Kemet, where the Nile's annual flooding would fertilize the soil with dark-brown silt. She wondered if this river flooded the same way, or if the winter rains were enough to sustain its farms.

Beyond the trees, along the river's opposite shore, arose a small hill on which stood a cluster of squarish white huts with thatched roofs. Between this village and the floodplain ran a stretch of grassland where herds of cattle and sheep milled about and grazed. Itaweret noticed that the cows all had short and stubby horns, instead of the long, lyre-curved horns of those bred in Kemet.

"I daresay these Achaean cows are pitifully small compared to ours," Bek muttered.

"That makes them less gluttonous, then," Gelon said, flashing a mean, side-eyed glare. He walked to one of the cows and gave her muzzle the gentle stroke of a man showing affection toward his favorite pet. "Isn't that the case, my sweet Helen?"

"That's quite a beauteous name for a big animal," Itaweret said. "It sounds like a pretty girl's name."

Philos laughed. "Leave it to a cowherd to treat his animals like princesses."

Gelon nodded. "Truth be told, I trust some animals more than I do some people. Especially those Kemetian melanchroides . . ."

Bek snarled and reached for his dagger. Itaweret pulled her brother away. "Stay your ground, lest you invoke the wrath of the entire village," she said. Truth be told, she wouldn't have minded clobbering Gelon with the scepter of Mut herself.

She turned to Philos with a disgusted grimace. "Is there anything we can do to douse that man's hatred for us?"

Philos shook his head with a sigh. "Don't worry yourself about him. Let's go meet my father."

They left Gelon with his cattle and walked up the path of dirt and trampled grass that led into the village, passing a primitive tower of branches and animal bones. From the thatch-roofed platform at its top, a sentry blew a harsh note through a ram's horn.

"Kemetians! What do you think you're doing here?" the man cried out, pointing a finger at Itaweret and Bek.

"They're guests of mine," Philos said. "They mean no harm."

The sentry grunted something unintelligible, although Itaweret thought she heard one of the same slurs Gelon had used earlier. The way he leered at her did not rub away her discomfort. Not in the least.

Nor did the crowd of Achaean villagers who hurried out of their huts to form a thick ring around her and Bek, staring through them with at least a hundred pairs of incredulous eyes while murmuring among themselves. Women hugged their infants and pulled their other children away, protecting them from the frightening foreigners . . . *beasts*. Some men stood in front of their wives and sisters, telling them to keep away from the Kemetian strangers. Several young males sprinkled the hostile looks with grinning, lecherous ogling directed at Itaweret. The younger women squinted and glowered a scintillating dislike toward her, more than their male counterparts.

"I think some of the local girls are a little bit jealous of your, ahem, foreign good looks, Itaweret," Philos spoke from the corner of his mouth.

Suddenly, the menacing circle of spectators parted. A gaunt, white-bearded man staggered toward Philos, the upper tip of his walking stick whittled into a bull's head. The gold circlet around the elder's balding head was a gleaming rare example of metal jewelry among the Achaeans; the others adorned themselves with simple strings of clay beads or animal fangs. He must be a king among primitives, Itaweret thought.

The old man regarded Itaweret and Bek with curious blinking and a sniffle. "I say, who are these black people you've brought among us, son of Metrophanes? They wouldn't be Kemetians from Per-Pehu, would they?"

Philos bowed his head. "Yes, my headman, but like I told the sentry, they mean no harm."

The headman shot a fierce, untrusting stare at Itaweret and Bek. "And you know this how? How do you know they aren't spies plotting an attack?"

"Oh, we wouldn't need spies to plan an attack on this place," Bek interjected. "The truth is, my sister Itaweret and I have come here as refugees. Per-Pehu has been sacked, and the remainder of its people enslaved."

"Who sacked it?" the headmaster asked.

"It was Scylax of Mycenae who attacked our city," Itaweret replied.

"Fitting comeuppance for those rapacious maurides, then!" one of the villagers shouted. Others cheered him on with waving fists.

Xiphos lowered himself to the ground, flattened his ears back, and growled. Philos hurried to stroke his back while begging him not to leap at anyone.

"Don't gloat for long over it," Itaweret told the villagers. "He is no less cruel than my ancestors were to yours. For all you know, he might come after your people next!"

"Why would he?" another villager said. "Your own brother said our 'hamlet' was too small, insignificant."

The headman balanced himself on his walking stick with both hands, his narrow eyes drifting in thought. He looked up to Itaweret, his thin lips stretched into a slight smile. He tapped the circlet on his head. "It was a Kemetian goldsmith who made this headband of mine," he said. "It is true that we have not always gotten along with the settlers at Per-Pehu. But don't we and the other villages have a tradition of trade with them? Have they not filled our granaries when our fields failed us? Let us not forget that it is the nature of Achaeans to be hospitable, as the gods of Olympus have decreed. I say we extend that hospitality to these refugees, Kemetian or not."

He turned to Itaweret and Bek. "Call me Damian, headman of Taurocephalus—the village of the bull's head. So long as my people listen to me, you've nothing to fear, my guests."

"I can only hope so," Itaweret said. "We're not planning to stay for long. Probably no more than overnight. So, Philos, where is the house of your father, Metrophanes?"

CHAPTER EIGHT

On the northwestern edge of the village, a hut squatted lower than the rest beneath the twisted branches of a mature oak tree. Alongside this simple dwelling leaned an even smaller shed of branches and thatch, with sheep and pig bones strewn underneath. After Philos rubbed Xiphos's mane, the lion retreated to this makeshift kennel to stretch and rest.

The hut's door opened. Out walked a woman of middle years, who laid a leg of roasted meat in front of Xiphos. In an instant, he snatched and tore into it with ravenous enthusiasm.

Philos grinned at Itaweret. "He likes to hunt on his own, but he appreciates my mother's cooking even more."

The older woman nodded with a chuckle. "Indeed, he does. And I am so glad to see both of you home. Did you find the missing ewe?"

"A bear got her, but Xiphos got him in turn. And I, um, brought a couple of guests with me. Itaweret and Bek, meet my mother, Rhea."

Rhea's squinting eyes widened over a dropped jaw as she examined the two Kemetians. "Why, by Zeus and all the other gods! What are . . . *they* doing over here, of all places?"

"We are refugees from Per-Pehu," Bek said. "We need shelter for the night."

Itaweret looked up to the tip of her scepter. "Plus, we believe there is something of great importance here. Our goddess Mut told us so."

Rhea crossed her arms. "What do you mean, your goddess told you there was something important here? We'll be more than happy to be your hosts, but this is a very strange turn of events."

Bek stretched his arms and shook his feet. "Let us explain later. We've been trudging through the wilds for two days, so we're rather worn out."

Rhea said nothing more as she opened the door and let them in. Inside, an earthy smell from the walls mingled with smoke from a hearth burning in the middle of the room. A tiny hole in the thatched roof gave the smoke escape. Benches ringed the fire; on one slept a plump man whose gray-striped beard suggested an age comparable to Rhea's. The moment the door closed, the man hauled himself onto his backside with a yawning groan and shook his head.

Rhea plucked a clay bottle from one of the shelves projecting from the walls and handed it to him. "Your son's home with company, so be nice."

Her husband took a swig from the bottle and let out a belch that a hippopotamus would envy. "Don't worry, I've heard it all through the door. Still a bit of a shocker to see Kemetians in this little cluster of mud huts, though."

Itaweret waved away the stench of his breath. "You're Metrophanes, aren't you?"

He smacked his lips. "Sorry to disappoint you. So, what's this I hear about the gods telling you something could be found in these parts?"

Itaweret took a seat across the hearth from Metrophanes, laid the scepter of Mut over her thighs, and brushed dust off its upper tip. "First, an explanation for why we're here. Our city, Per-Pehu, has fallen to King Scylax of Mycenae. He's sacked it and enslaved everyone he hasn't slain."

Silence hung in the room as Metrophanes lowered his head, his lips moving without speech. The bottle slipped from his fingers and crashed onto the floor, spilling what remained of the wine. His eyes glistened. "I should have known . . . I shouldn't have left it to him . . ."

Bek leaned toward him. "Left *what* to him? To whom?"

Rising to his feet, Metrophanes laid his hands on Philos and Rhea's shoulders. "I never would have thought I'd need to tell any of you this, but . . . Scylax . . . is my brother. My younger brother."

A quivering Philos stepped back from his father, the color draining from his face momentarily, receding like a tide. It reared up and returned in a full force of reddened fury. "How could you . . . hide something like that from everyone? From me?"

"And how did you end up a mere shepherd's father, anyway?" Bek asked.

Metrophanes sighed. "Philos, I told you that I was abducted by bandits on a hunting trip and then sold into slavery, until I earned my freedom back and wandered over here, where we had you. All that is true. What I did not tell you is what my life was like before that happened. I was king of Mycenae before Scylax.

"And what a burden it was! You may imagine kingship to be a life of luxury and power, but no. It is a life restrained by responsibility and plagued with anxious distrust. You see, I was never the most popular with my own court. The people loved me, sure, for I did everything I could to rule with justice, compassion, and charity—"

"Why would your courtiers dislike you for that?" Itaweret asked. "Some of our pharaohs back in Kemet would envy you for your nobility."

Metrophanes picked up a few shards of the broken bottle and rubbed them together, as if they were silver coins. "The thing is, if you are king, benevolence is expensive. And if you are to spend your treasury on behalf of the poor and helpless, whence must your taxes come? From the wealthy and well-off, of course!"

Bek grunted. "It's like my father used to say. No one cries about being taxed more than those who have plenty to spare."

Metrophanes laughed—which started a fit of coughing. After hacking for a half-minute, he caught his breath. "Tell me about it! Not a day went by without me hearing some pampered bastard telling me I was too generous, not to mention too soft and cowardly. What they respect is what they see as strength, what they see as courage, and what they think will make them yet richer. What they wanted was a conquering and pillaging warrior, a man like Scylax."

"Do you think it could have been Scylax who had something to do with those bandits who captured you?" Itaweret said. "If he had your court's favor, they—or possibly the man himself—could have hired them to get rid of you and have him take your place."

Metrophanes shrugged. "I've considered that but cannot prove it. It doesn't matter anyway. I've no intention of going back to Mycenae."

Itaweret gasped, rose to her feet, and clenched her scepter. "You mean, you're simply going to let Scylax go around, wiping out cities and dragging entire chunks of humanity into bondage?"

"Don't misunderstand me like that, young lady! I don't approve of what Scylax has done to your people any more than anyone else. But how, by Hades, could I possibly take my throne back from him? You'd have to be a fool if you think I can talk old Damian into rallying the village against the might of Mycenae!"

"Then why not speak to leaders from one of the other Achaean cities?" Bek said. "There's got to be at least one that can stand up to Scylax."

Metrophanes shook his head. "That's assuming he hasn't befriended them already. He's always wanted all Achaeans to unite into one mighty empire. What you'd need against that force is an even bigger one."

Philos snapped his fingers. "Like the Trojans! They're surely big enough to conquer Scylax if they wanted to. All we'd have to do is cross the Great Green to the east and ask for their aid."

Metrophanes shook his head with a frustrated groan. "Don't be silly, boy. You've neither the skills of a sailor nor the tongue of a diplomat. Oh, and you barely even know how to manage a herd of sheep, never mind a kingdom of men. Do you seriously see yourself as inheriting any throne from me?"

"Look, I am the son of Per-Pehu's great chief," Bek said. "I believe I've studied enough statecraft to teach it to your son. And if nobody else here knows the tongue, I can speak to the Trojans on his behalf. You have nothing stopping you from taking back what's rightfully yours, Metrophanes."

Metrophanes waddled over to the shelf and reached for another bottle of wine. Rhea pulled his arm away before he could lay a finger on the bottle. She slapped him across the cheek. "You've had enough, husband. You can't drink this all away. Is that the example you want to set for our son?"

With a deep breath, Metrophanes walked to the opposite side of the room. He pried open a cedar chest and withdrew a necklace of red beads, its centerpiece a twinkling disk of gold. He gave it to Philos. "This was mine, and my father's before me. It's yours now."

Philos slipped on the necklace and ran his finger over its pendant. "This is the symbol of Mycenae, isn't it?"

Metrophanes smiled. "Only a king may wear it. I am much too old to fight for anything anymore. So, I shall leave it to you, my son."

Philos stammered as he fondled the circle of gold. "Me . . . fight . . . to be king . . . but, Father . . . why?"

"You are my son, are you not? A king's son follows in his father's footsteps. Your new friend Bek's wisdom as a statesman and warrior should help you with leading the kingdom and its armies."

"But, still, it's so much . . . responsibility. Too much. There is no way that I, I—" Philos ran out of the hut, leaving the door swinging back and forth on its hinge.

Itaweret felt the scepter of Mut emit a cozy warmth into the palms of her hands. *Well done, my priestess. Henceforth begins the true quest.*

The shorter, stouter sibling of the hill that supported Taurocephalus spread to the west. Philos retreated to it and sprinted around the cypresses that stood on its slope before perching himself on the lone boulder on its summit. He'd traveled the route on many evenings to admire a sunset behind the mountains, and then the stars and moon that lit the heavens in the sun's place, while listening to the chirp of crickets as another man might listen to the village bard's songs. Given his father's stunning revelation, and everything else that had just happened, he knew nowhere else to go.

Philos now knew that, were his father to challenge Scylax for his former throne and prevail, he would have no choice but to inherit that throne. One could never be king without passing it down to their eldest son. That's how kingship worked in almost every civilization. In most cases, it made sense, as a king could teach his heir how to rule in the way most parents would teach the family trade to their children. Except for one thing: Metrophanes waited until now, after Philos's twenty-fifth summer, to reveal the truth, rather than beginning the training early in his life.

Metrophanes taught Philos another trade—how to herd sheep. Philos shook his head. How could he lead an entire army against the strongest of all the Achaean cities, never mind govern an entire city of several thousand men and women, when he couldn't even prevent one ewe from running away and getting eaten by a bear?

Moreover, could he forgive Metrophanes? Should he? Old though Metrophanes was, his father should have done more to prepare him. Or, at the very least, agree to join his son and the two Kemetians on their adventure. Instead, the fat old drunk chose to wallow like a bloated pig in his hut while throwing Philos into a danger and responsibility beyond his ability to handle.

It was selfish. Cowardly. Behavior unworthy of a true king of Mycenae.

Philos screamed in anger as he hurled a fallen branch like a javelin into the violet sky. Vulgarities raced from his mouth, the echoes so loud that even Xiphos would cower and whimper were he to hear his master's voice. It did no good. The volcanic explosion only exhausted him and wore his voice hoarse. Philos fell back onto the rock like it was his bed and broke down into a storm of tears.

"Are you all right, Philos?"

Itaweret sat down on the rock next to him. Her eyes sparkled brighter than any stars beginning to speckle the sky.

"Sorry for the unmanly display I have put up here. I don't cry like this most times."

Itaweret wiped a tear off his cheek with a long finger, its two rings reflecting the light of far distant stars. "Everyone cries from time to time, even if they don't show it to anyone else. And I don't blame you in the least."

"Thank the gods, you don't. Blame my father. He's the one who forced this all onto me. Why won't he come along with us?"

"I know how you feel. But has your father not grown old and worn himself out? I don't see a man in his current shape lasting a single night beyond this village. I wouldn't trust him to lead Bek and me through those woods and mountains like you did."

The forests that dressed the mountains on both sides of the valley were darker than the sky itself. The eerie cry of a distant wolf howled from somewhere within them.

Philos shook his head. "It wasn't that hard with Xiphos at my side."

"That's the thing, though. As long as you have him—and Bek, and me—at your side, you don't have nearly as much to worry about as you think."

"It's not only the peril that I fear. There's so much that a king must do for his people, to take care of so many. He's like a father to thousands upon thousands! You expect me to manage all of that, without even the smallest bit of experience?"

"You know my brother said he will show you how to run everything. Our father was the great chief of our city, and Bek studied his whole life to follow in his footsteps."

"Wait, wait, Bek's only *studied* how to rule a city? He's never done it himself? He must be very 'helpful,' then!"

"Philos, stop making excuses—"

"Then stop trying to get me to do this all for you!"

Philos scooted to the far end of the rock and looked away from her. As far as he was concerned, Itaweret and Bek brought all of this on. It was their fault that this would befall him. He should have left them to the bear instead of troubling himself with their plight.

"If that's how you feel, I guess Bek and I will have to take on Scylax without your help," Itaweret said. "We're not letting him go unpunished. Not when he has the rest of our people in chains!"

"Look, it's not like I don't want things to get better for you and your people," Philos said. "It's simply that I'm not the one to do it. Find somebody else."

"You heard the rest of your village. They don't even want us here. Philos, you're the only one here we can trust with our lives. You aren't like the others. You're far better than them."

"Even if that were true, I'm only one man. How could I do everything that's being asked of me?"

Itaweret ran her fingers along the tip of her scepter. "You won't be alone. None of us will. Remember, I am a priestess of Mut. As long as she is watching over us, we should have nothing to fear."

"So, all you have is faith? You know how fickle gods and goddesses can be. What if your Mut were to let us down somehow?"

"She won't, trust me. The gods of Kemet are nothing like what is said of your gods. Especially not Mut, whose benevolence knows no bounds. You can count on her."

Philos shrugged and groaned, exhausted. No way of talking her out of this. He felt himself being dragged into her mission, no matter how many counter arguments he presented. Maybe it would be less trouble to cave in. Come to think of it . . . he might even get something out of this after all. Between his loins rose the same warm, tense sensation he felt the moment he first laid eyes on the Kemetian girl.

"On second thought, I'll be more than eager to help out," Philos said. "On one condition. You know how a king always needs his queen, don't you?"

Itaweret grimaced. "I know what you're talking about . . ."

"No, wait—"

The priestess strode away, leaving Philos by himself. Even as she disappeared into the darkness, headed back to the village, he could not take his eyes off her. If ever there were an opportunity to court the girl, this was it . . . the two of them talking about a plan, sharing their concerns and fears, Itaweret spurring on his courage, him looking into her eyes and seeing not only her beauty but her strength and resolve.

Now, he'd blown it. He would never forgive himself.

A little gust blew on his scalp. *Whoosh.* Overhead, an owl flapped its wings, hovering as it watched, its bright eyes an unnatural silver-gray. Philos had heard stories of bewitching owls, but he could not place when or where, or what the mysterious birds were really supposed to be.

After a single hoot, the owl vanished without the slightest trace.

CHAPTER NINE

The village sentry's horn blared through Itaweret's dreams like a stone smashing fine pottery. She rose from a wall bench inside the hut of Metrophanes. The glow of the central hearth's fire and screens of morning sunlight beamed through the crevices between the door's wooden planks. Rhea was already up, cooking over the hearth until the horn blew again. The wife of Metrophanes stopped in mid-stir. "Sounds like we have more visitors."

Itaweret sprang to the next bench and prodded a sleeping Bek on the back with both hands. "We've got to get up. It could be trouble."

Her brother's eyelids snapped open. "Already? I was hoping we'd catch a break for once."

After Itaweret helped him up, they burst through the door—and stumbled upon a glimmering wall of bronze and boar-tusk helmeted soldiers posted along the front yard. Well over three dozen soldiers were armed with spears and the double-domed cowhide shields of Mycenae. Before them stood an Achaean woman around Rhea's age, wearing a wolf skin as a hooded shawl over her gown. On one finger of her raised hand, an owl with radiant silver-gray eyes perched. *I've seen that owl*, Itaweret thought.

The wolf-skin woman greeted Itaweret with a sinister sneer. "Well, if it isn't the daughter of Mahu, former great chief of Per-Pehu . . ."

Itaweret's fingers wrapped tight around the scepter of Mut until her knuckles almost turned white under her dark skin. "'Former'? What happened to him?"

"Ooh, I forgot, you weren't there to see my little brother Scylax finish him and his wife off. Such a pity."

A furious growl arose from deep within Itaweret. Snarling like a provoked leopard, she started to lunge at the Mycenaean woman until Rhea grabbed her by the shoulders. "Kleno, you callous bitch! I'll have you pummeled into paste when I—"

Kleno threw her head back and cackled. "Such bold talk from a pampered young priestess. I'll make it quick. You turn yourself over to me, along with your brother, and all these people shall live with nary a scratch!"

"You mean that you're going to kill all these innocent people if you don't have us?" Bek asked. "Why should we even entertain such terrible demands?"

"You aren't the village chief around here, are you? What gives you the right to speak on these farmers' behalf?"

Old Damian approached through the morning mist, a gold band gleaming on his walking stick. "No, this Kemetian is not the headman around here," he said. "I am. And you have no right to barge in here with your minions, threatening violence over a couple of refugees! Do you understand that, Mycenaean witch?"

More villagers gathered in a semicircle behind the Mycenaeans. Many men and a few women carried wooden clubs and staffs, rakes, hoes, and copper-pointed spears, forming a fence of crude weaponry at their front ranks. One among them did not possess the same wary glint in his eyes . . . Gelon, the cowherd. "You sure we shouldn't simply hand that melanchroides woman and her brother over to them?" he asked. "What have those Kemetians done for us?"

"Silence, Gelon!" Damian said. "No matter our guests' race or country of origin, there is a thing known as common decency. Remember, they've done nothing *against* us, either."

"But why should we care what happens to them either way? They're not our people. They could *never* be our people."

Kleno snapped her fingers three times. "Enough of this bickering! I won't say it again. Offer the two Kemetians to our custody, and we'll be off!"

Itaweret recognized the same dilemma as when Scylax visited her father in Per-Pehu. The very notion of surrendering her freedom to Scylax, Kleno, or any Mycenaean jackal was more loathsome than before. Now she knew what they had done in Per-Pehu. The Mycenaeans had done it because she refused Scylax's advances.

Blood spilled and her people found themselves slain or enslaved, all because of her. She didn't want to cause any more suffering for the villagers of Taurocephalus.

The door to the hut flung open. Out waddled Metrophanes, wrath sparkling in his eyes despite his half-drunken stupor. Kleno paled and took two steps back from him. "Metrophanes! I never would have—"

"At least you were able to recognize me after all these years, big sister," Metrophanes said. "Now you know those bandits didn't kill me, like you and Scylax probably thought. While I have no way of proving whether you or Scylax had anything to do with that abduction, what I have learned is the damage he's done in my absence. Since you know now that I have never been dead, I want my throne back!"

Itaweret nodded. "I'd listen to him if I were you, Kleno. You will only disgrace yourself if you have his blood on your hands."

Kleno looked around, and then whispered to her owl. The bird hooted, its eyes burning in their brightest gleam of silver gray. The owl soared from its priestess's finger, swooped down onto Metrophanes's head, and punctured his scalp with her talons. The bird then carried him away with far greater strength than any bird of its size should have possessed, his screams puncturing the distant fog. Itaweret stared in stunned silence.

Once Metrophanes's hollering trailed off, only the gasping breaths of the villagers remained audible. All eyes drifted back to Kleno, whose smug grin showed not one sign of remorse over her little brother's death.

"How could you do that?" Bek asked. "That was your brother!"

"I wouldn't aggravate the situation even more, young Kemetian," Kleno said. "For the last time, give yourselves over and we'll leave everyone else here alone."

"I'd sooner rot in the abyss of Duat than let you touch my sister or me!"

"Is that so? Then to the abyss you and all your hosts go!"

Kleno snapped her fingers again. Her entourage turned to face the villagers behind them with a terrible clatter of plated armor. The people of Taurocephalus answered with a savage, collective whooping cry, attacking the soldiers with their makeshift weaponry. Copper and bronze banged against each other, wood scratched and smashed over shields and breastplates, and the sharp ends of spears pierced through flesh and cracked bone. The odors of gore swamped over the crisp morning with the sudden fury of a flash flood.

Itaweret could not watch the innocent villagers die without doing anything. She had to act.

She screamed the Kemetian battle cry, her voice steep and shrill, then swung her scepter onto a Mycenaean soldier's head. It smashed through the ivory platelets of his helmet to his skull, the resulting eruption of blood and brain fluid soaking his hair. An eager roar rose from the resisting villagers as they watched him crumple to his death.

Many times, Itaweret had play-fought Bek with sticks. Only on occasion had she drawn blood in those childish spars, never intentionally. Now was the first moment she fought to injure a man. And kill him. Many would have been repulsed, horrified, later scarred.

She relished it.

The Mycenaeans wheeled around toward her and charged, their spears thrust forward. Sweeping the scepter of Mut sideways, Itaweret knocked down one soldier with a blow to his cheekbone. He collapsed onto his fallen comrade. The soldiers toppled over each other like a row of dominoes.

Itaweret twirled the scepter about, yipping like a hyena on the hunt, until a Mycenaean began parrying her with his sword. Sparks shot out where the blade clashed with the copper shaft. She recoiled from the vibrating force of the attack.

A smaller flash of copper whirred through the air and plunged into the warrior's face. Bek's dagger.

He picked up a sword from one of the fallen Mycenaeans. "You didn't think I'd let you have all the fun, did you, Sister?"

Itaweret smiled through a wild-eyed, fierce expression. "I wasn't counting on it."

She raised her scepter to knock out another soldier's brains. Before she could bring it down, Kleno's owl seized it with bloodied claws. Itaweret's arm muscles stretched in her struggle to pull the scepter out of the bird's grasp, but the owl flapped its wings in a furious frenzy, dragging her behind, along with her weapon. Her heels dug into the earth, almost losing contact with the ground until her hands slipped off. The owl taunted her with a screech as she landed on her backside.

Over the din of battle and massacre, a roar. *Xiphos.* The lion grabbed the scepter in his long teeth and pried it out of the owl's talons, bringing down the bird as well. He swung his head, released his jaw, and flung the scepter to Itaweret as Philos ran over to help her up.

"Where were you two all this time?" Itaweret asked. "You sure could have come in handy."

"I was out taking Xiphos for a walk," Philos said. "Speaking of Xiphos—*no!*"

The lion roared at the Mycenaean ranks—and charged. He lunged a paw at one soldier, who blocked him with his shield and then cut a glancing wound across the lion's shoulder with his spear.

Philos whistled and clapped his hands. "Xiphos, stay back! Those men are armored. You'll get yourself killed!"

"If we can't take advantage of your pet, what do we do?" Bek asked.

"We hurry out of here. There's nothing more we can do."

"You can't be serious!" Itaweret said. "You can't let your own family die like this!"

"As far as I can see, they're already all dead. I saw that owl with my father on the way here. As for my mother . . ."

Philos pointed to a body strewn over the village's gore-flooded streets. Itaweret turned. It was Rhea, a dripping red hole through her breast. Nearby lay Damian, the headman, still holding onto half of his walking-stick.

A few fighting villagers remained within the mass of Mycenaean spearmen, but their numbers became even fewer with every blinking moment. Already, some of the huts' thatched roofs had gone up in flames, that of Philos and his family among them.

The sting of smoke brought tears to Itaweret's eyes. And much more. Again, an entire community had fallen into bloody and burning ruin before her eyes. And again, it had all happened over her.

She, Bek, Philos, and his lion fled without a single glance back.

CHAPTER TEN

They reached the foothills beyond the valley's eastern verge and plunged into the woods. If anything could protect them from Mycenaean eyes, it was the cover of the trees. The darkness of the upland forest, which Itaweret had found so forbidding, now stood as the closest thing to safety, especially compared with the flat, sun-lit expanse of the valley plains behind them.

She leaned against the trunk of an oak and panted while running her hands down her strained calves. A whole morning spent fighting and fleeing had worn her body sore and dried out her throat. Not even the moisture from her last drink at the valley stream remained.

Bek brushed the sweat off his face. "We should have thought to bring some waterskins. Or make them ourselves. Philos, you wouldn't happen to know where we could find a pool among these hills, would you?"

Philos was nowhere to be found. Bek called out his name several times, each louder than the last. Only the birds answered, with panicked squawks and fluttering.

Bek threw a stone against a pine. "The coward! He must have left us to save his own skin."

"Don't be silly," Itaweret said. "Where would he go without us? He's got to be nearby."

A muffled yell broke through the taciturn woods. It was not the roar of a savage beast, but the hollering of a young man. The same voice she heard during the night. She pointed to sandal-shaped tracks that ran in a crooked trail deeper into the forest. "Those have to be his. Why don't we follow them?"

They ran down the path of prints, the stench of death growing stronger, the same smell as the carcass of the slain bear. Had Philos died? His scream sounded more angry than frightened, though, let alone like a death rattle. Then she thought of a darker possibility . . . had he taken his own life?

She found him. Alive. By the body of another man, Xiphos at his side. The man's skull and eye sockets bled rivers of blood from cranial puncture wounds. She did not need to examine the body to identify him. *Metrophanes.* Philos's plaintive sobbing said everything. The lion's mane grew wetter by the minute, catching his master's tears.

Itaweret sat next to Philos. "You've lost everything, haven't you?"

"All within four days. My family . . . my people . . . my whole damned world. It's all gone. All thanks to those demons from Mycenae!"

"It's like what happened to us, Philos. Scylax has taken away everything we hold dear."

"Then to the darkest depths of the underworld with him! I can't let him get away with this!"

Rising to his feet, a furious determination flickering loud and moist in his teary eyes, Philos picked up a long branch from the undergrowth and banged its end on the ground the way Itaweret's father would have banged his great chief's scepter. He nodded toward her. "Itaweret and Bek, you shall have my aid," he said.

Bek waved his fist in the air. "That's the spirit, Philos. Though I must wonder, how are we going to get all the way to Troy from here? Sister, could you consult Mut on this?"

Itaweret gripped the goddess's scepter with both hands and closed her eyes. Warmth pulsated from the copper shaft into her palms, coursing through her body like the blood in her veins. The throbbing of her heart accelerated into a frenetic ritual drumbeat, the voices of priestesses chanting to the rhythm of her breathing.

Moments later, Mut reared before her, the glossy black figure draped in gold as scintillating as the sun itself. Her voice carried a musical resonance. "You have done well so far, my high priestess. Now awaits the next step of your journey. But I must warn you, Itaweret, that it won't be as simple as you expect."

"What do you mean? We've found the next king of Mycenae. All we need is an army strong enough to back him up against Scylax. That is why we're headed for Troy."

"And yet you do not know if the Trojans will listen to your pleas. Nor do you know how to even get to Troy," the goddess uttered.

"We could find someone to take us there. There are plenty of merchants plying the waters between Achaea and Troy, aren't there?"

"Yet you have not even the smallest amount to pay them with. No merchant will escort you for free. You need some way to persuade them. I will give you one clue to find your way. Seek out he who distrusts you most. He is closer than you know . . ."

The goddess faded into the darkness, followed by the drums and chanting, the rhythmic sound trailing into silence. The heat within Itaweret dissipated.

She opened her eyes to find the world as she had left it. "'Seek out he who distrusts you most' . . . that's what she told me."

Bek scoffed. "That's helpful. These gods sure like to give clear and unambiguous instructions." His voice resonated with sarcasm.

"Could she mean someone working for Scylax?" Philos asked. "They don't exactly like us."

Itaweret sighed and shook her head. "No, but they don't exactly have any reason to *distrust* us either. It must be someone who thinks we're up to no good. The only one I can think of is . . . but where would we find him?"

"Who are you talking about?"

"Gelon, your cowherd friend. He showed nothing but prejudice and hostility toward us. If that isn't distrust, I don't know what else to call it."

"Hold up, hold up!" Bek said. "Even assuming he made it out of that massacre alive, what could that smelly warthog of a man do for us?"

"I guess we'll have to find out once we track him down." She turned to Philos. "How can we track him? Where would he go?"

Philos snapped his fingers. "I know one place we might be able to find him, though I can't promise it. But there is one thing I want to do before we leave."

He knelt again beside the body of Metrophanes, placing a hand on the dead man's breast and murmuring phrases under his breath. With his other hand, Philos clutched the gold pendant of the necklace Metrophanes had given him.

"I wish to build a pyre for my father," Philos said. "And then bury his bones. May Hades watch over him in the calm gloom of the underworld."

Itaweret had always thought the Achaean view of the underworld a dreary, depressing place, like that of the other eastern peoples. Her people saw the underworld as merely a place through which the departed passed before arriving at the hall of Osiris for his judgment. Afterward, these departed souls would enjoy the eternal splendor and bliss of the afterlife if they were found worthy. By contrast, as far as she knew, the northern and eastern cultures always seemed to equate the darkness of the underworld with the afterlife itself, as if they did not look forward to or envision an eternal place of joy after death.

Disagree as she might, it was not the time to question Philos's worldview. She could only help him with his request. She smiled. "And may his spirit watch over you, together with all your ancestors."

A pair of Kemetian obelisks stabbed at the sky, taller than the pines from opposite sides of the mountain pass. There, the Mycenaean army set up. Three centuries of wind and winter rains had weathered away the hieroglyphic texts that ran down the pyramid-topped monoliths. No matter. Scylax did not need to read them to know they marked the eastern colonial boundary of Per-Pehu. He would have his men knock them down and the slaves drag them to Mycenae, where he could exhibit them before his palace as yet more trophies of his conquest. Or perhaps the Kemetian captives could do the toppling instead. The only drawback would be the wasted time and strength, both of which could be better spent on greater plans.

Speaking of trophies, where was his biggest prize of sacking Per-Pehu, Itaweret? It wasn't like Kleno to take so many days carrying out his wishes. Had that Kemetian harlot somehow evaded even Athena's keen vision? Did she even live anymore? *You had better not have killed Itaweret, Kleno*, Scylax thought. Disobeying his order like that would leave him no choice but to treat her the way he had treated their brother long ago.

Scylax's lieutenant jogged over from the camp's far exit, a scroll of papyrus in his hand. "Sorry to be the bearer of bad news, my king . . ."

Scylax stopped gnawing a pig bone and threw it into the campfire. "Don't tell me something happened to Kleno."

"So far, still no word from her, I'm afraid. But that's not the bad news. The bad news, Your Highness, is that there's been a riot in Mycenae. Were it not for our guards' prompt action, they could have torn your statue down!"

"Oh, for the love of Zeus! I will give this to old Metrophanes. He was good at getting 'the people' to shut up!"

"Forgive me for saying this, my dear king, but maybe it's how you've handled the treasury that's the issue? You must admit that you've been spending far more on wars like this than on, say, feeding the poor and needy . . ."

Scylax stomped his foot. "I'm not going to have this conversation. For the thousandth time, if I must tax and spend on anything, it will be on making us stronger and more secure, not on pampering those who won't help themselves. And besides, lieutenant, you know we're carrying back a mountain's worth of loot. Some of that wealth is bound to eventually flow into the pockets of the poor, even if it comes in the smallest trickle. War is always good for a nation's wealth."

A Kemetian slave girl carried a jug on her head as she walked toward the two men. With a resentful frown, she poured wine into their goblets before striding away.

The lieutenant took a swig. "I daresay I find this whole attitude of yours about war rather ironic. Was it not war that took Erastos's life?"

Scylax blew out a mouthful of wine. His face flared a bright flaming red as the memories swarmed back. Not even the tears that dripped from the corners of his eyes could douse the heat on his cheek. "You will not use my father's death against me!" he said. "Not after it shaped me into the man I am today. My brother thought he could bring peace by avoiding war altogether. He was a spineless fool! The only way you can bring peace to this cruel world is by fighting the greatest war of all. Once one king and one king alone brings the world together, then there will be peace. But first, that king must fight for it!"

"Fair enough," the lieutenant said. "I'll leave you in peace for the night."

Scylax drank what remained of the wine. It did not taste as sweet as usual. It was difficult to savor even the most delicious drink when recalling his father's mutilated body blooming into flame on the pyre.

Don't you ever feel left out, my son. The voice of Erastos echoed within Scylax's head. *I may have to prepare your brother for kingship and your sister for the priesthood, but I love you all the same.*

Was it true?

Scylax never found out. He did know he was the one who got into the most trouble, always scolded and talked down to by others. All because he was the last-born, following Kleno and Metrophanes. If only he could make up his foolishness and troublemaking to his father . . .

It was never to be. Erastos left for the abode of Hades before Scylax saw his twentieth summer. Never would his father see how strong his youngest had grown, nor how he would forge the mightiest empire the world had ever known. Or would ever know. Then Erastos would understand how his neglect had become his folly.

No use in dwelling on what could have been. What mattered now was the mission that lay ahead. He could no longer make his father proud, so instead he would make all of Mycenae proud. And his own children as well.

First, however, he needed a queen. A certain dark, Kemetian queen. He was growing tired of waiting for her.

CHAPTER ELEVEN

Evening returned to the valley, a glow of dark red stretching from a hill that jutted above the river's eastern bank, south of where Taurocephalus had once stood. Unlike most of the other little rises that broke up the otherwise flat valley floor, the hill's western face featured a rugged cliff. A cave yawned into the rock like a giant mouth with stone teeth. Gelon stepped into its mouth and retreated for the night with a torch he fashioned from nearby wood.

Everyone in the village had known about the cave for ages, but most shunned it. Gelon would have done the same had he not once followed Philos during a boyhood game of chase. Philos had always been the more adventurous, the one most willing to go out and take risks. Maybe that, more than anything else, drew him to the two Kemetian melanchroides. In bringing those black demons home, he brought about the destruction of the village he and Gelon had always called home.

Gelon shook his head and kicked a rock across the cave floor. To think he had ever considered that fool his closest friend! The rock clanked over the stone surface, the sound echoing across the darkness, but no other sound answered it. Gelon sighed with relief. If there were any lions, bears, or other denning carnivores, they would have growled. Wouldn't they?

As he advanced further, a cold prickle ran down the back of Gelon's neck. The fire of the torch, his only buffer against the pitch blackness, dimmed with every waver of its yellow tongues. While halting to check his surroundings, something scuffled from elsewhere in the cavern.

Gelon tumbled onto his backside with a yelp. As his torch rolled out of his hands, its light fell onto the snarling face of a lioness . . .

was it real? He mustered the courage to look more closely. No, not a real, flesh-and-blood animal . . . but a drawing painted on the wall with red ocher. Nor was it an isolated doodle. Paintings and drawings covered the passageway from floor to low ceiling, works faded by their age, which nobody knew. He recognized deer, wild cattle, horses, bears, lions, and wolves. However, other paintings portrayed more fanciful creatures he could not identify—stocky and hairy beasts with horns sticking out of their snouts, hunched dog-like animals with spotted coats, and big lynx-like cats with oversized upper fangs. Least familiar of all were the giant, shaggy animals with long, curving tusks and elongated, snake-like noses drooping down from their faces like proboscises.

Interspersed between the animals were the painted outlines of human hands, as well as human stick figures with spears and bows and arrows. Gelon knew which people these ancient drawings represented. This was the work of the old Pelasgians, the people who had lived in Achaea before the Achaeans themselves.

"This animal with the big tusks looks like an elephant . . . but ours have bigger ears and aren't so hairy . . ."

A voice. A cloudy voice. He stepped back.

Muffled though the voice was, he could never mistake its thick, exotic accent. Those cursed Kemetians had somehow followed him! The light glowing from behind a turn in the passage gave their presence away. He had to run, even if he sprinted all the way into the underworld . . .

Wait. Best to confront them. Eliminate them once and for all. Or die trying.

Gelon charged with a battle cry, brandishing his torch like a club. "Stay back, you filthy black devils! Or I shall kill you both!"

A fist crashed into his breast, throwing him back onto the cave floor. Philos stood over him, tearing the torch out of his grip. "Calm down, Gelon!"

"I ought to kill you too, Philos. You betrayed us all. This all happened because of you!"

Gelon pounced at Philos, but a dark arm shot out and wrested him away by the throat. Next came a blood-stained copper dagger, which slid over the skin of Philos's neck.

Bek threw Gelon down. "There are three of us and one of you. The only way you're getting out of this alive is if you cooperate."

"Why should I?" Gelon said. "You took everything I ever knew from me. Everything!"

Itaweret knelt by him and offered her hand. "No, it was Scylax of Mycenae. This all happened because of that tyrant. He is the one who destroyed our home. And he, through his sister Kleno, is the one who destroyed yours as well. We all have the same enemy here. Now please, I implore you, trust us this once."

Were these Kemetians telling the truth? Gelon had no way of knowing. Neither did he have a safer way out. With a nervous wince, he touched Itaweret's dark hand and let her pull him back onto his footing.

"I have to say, all these cave paintings are quite beautiful," Itaweret said. "Did your ancestors make them?"

Gelon blushed faintly from the flattery. "Nope. These would be the work of the Pelasgians before us."

"They remind me of some of the drawings our own ancestors drew onto rocks, back when Kemet beyond the Nile was a grassy savanna rather than desert. Some of the animals even look like the ones we knew. Hyenas, lions, rhinoceroses, even those elephant-looking creatures."

Bek pointed to one of the painted horses. "Not to mention, the zebras in these don't seem to have any stripes."

"Well, I'd be lying if I didn't come here from time to time to appreciate the paintings," Gelon said. "It makes for a great resting spot after a busy day of herding cattle in the sun. Is that really why you're here?"

"We need your help," Philos said. "We're not going to let Scylax continue his reign of terror anymore. Not without a fight. Our plan is to go to Troy and have their army beat his on our behalf."

Gelon stared at his old friend, incredulous. "All the way to Troy? By the gods, you can't be serious. I bet none of you can even row a canoe all the way across a river!"

"We're not planning to row there ourselves, you dumb ox," Bek said. "We're going to buy our way over there. And we've been told you know where to find the payment."

Gelon scratched his chin with a finger. "We do know there's a Phoenician port to the south where the river touches the coast. And we know the Phoenicians take their payment in silver. Now, where are you going to get silver?"

Itaweret squinted and pointed to the far side of the tunnel. "What's that over there?"

The painting she indicated did not portray animals, human beings, or even human hands. Instead, it showed a circle of black vertical dashes, supported by horizontal dashes on top, that enclosed a cluster of pale gray dots. When exposed to the torchlight, the dots in the middle glistened like silver.

Gelon ran his hand over them. Some of the silver paint rubbed onto his fingertips. "The legends were true all along . . . I think I know where to find your payment."

CHAPTER TWELVE

A narrow series of steps, worn and cracked from unknown age, scaled up and along the face of another cliff overlooking the valley's southeastern edge. They ran at least a hundred feet from bottom to top. Itaweret could not look away from the cliff as she followed Gelon up the primitive stairs. To do so would scare her into falling off.

Behind her, Bek walked sideways while keeping his hands on the rock to the side. "If these Pelasgians were smart enough to carve out steps like this, they should have thought to build a railing along them, too."

Philos brought up the rear, with Xiphos hopping behind him. "Maybe that rotted away. Who knows?"

If anything had kept Itaweret's mind off the exerting task of walking up the steps, it was a story Gelon had told her the previous night about the Pelasgians—the ancient people who called the entire country home before the ancestors of the Achaeans arrived from the east. They did not plant crops or keep livestock but rather lived off the land as hunters and gatherers. They slept in huts of timber, hide, and the bones of great beasts, and they worshiped in caves much like the one in which they found Gelon. They would have painted the images on the cave walls. And chiseled the steps into the cliff face.

The detail Itaweret found most fascinating was Gelon's description of the Pelasgians. Clad in animal skins, their skin would have been almost as dark as her own people, yet their eyes were as blue as the sky. Itaweret had heard legends of white-skinned men in the farthest north with blue eyes and yellow hair, but never a darker-skinned race with that peculiar eye color. Even the Achaeans possessed the same dark eyes as almost every other race she had seen.

Beyond the upper lip of the cliff where the steps ended, a grassy field spread beneath the twilit sky, more like the valley floor than the wooded highlands terrain. Except for a couple of oaks and carobs, almost no trees stood on the plateau.

From its center rose a knoll like a giant dome, surrounded by irregular stone pillars that each dwarfed an elephant in height if not weight. Some of the megaliths stood in pairs that supported a third stone between them like lintels for oversized doorways. Into the faces of the blocky columns were inscribed images of wild animals in a style reminiscent of the cave paintings, except these carvings sparkled with traces of silver paint.

"You want me to believe that savages who lived like animals erected these?" Bek said. "The very first rulers of Kemet would have envied them!"

Gelon raised an eyebrow. "Savages, you say? And you maurides have the gall to complain that *I* am prejudiced against you."

Philos called out his friend's name with a stern frown. The conversation ended there.

A human-sized hole bore into the central mound's slope, framed with rocks. Poles of wood and bone formed a grille blocking its entrance, with a disk of corroded silver mounted on it. Itaweret brushed away some of the mold that clung to the disk's surface, exposing a swirling, coiled design in the moonlight. The design ended on one side with the fanged jaws of a serpent-like reptile.

A red glint flashed over the gemstone embedded into the illustrated creature's eye socket, followed by a deep growling hiss.

Itaweret shuddered, her skin turning even colder than the night air. "Anyone hear that?"

The others shot blank looks of incredulity her way. Bek glanced over his shoulder, clutching the hilt of his dagger, and grunted with a shrug. "Is something bothering you, Sister?"

"Oh, nothing. Maybe it was Xiphos."

The lion cocked his head with a confused moan. Philos patted him on the head. "In case it was, we'll be standing outside. Wouldn't want to spook our friends, would we, Xiphos?"

After the shepherd escorted his pet away, Bek grabbed the silver disk with both hands, pulled it off the wooden grille, his arm muscles stretching and bunching, and tossed it onto the ground. The instant it landed, it did not bang or whir like a normal metal disk but hissed like a provoked cobra. Itaweret leaped to her brother's side with a yelp.

Gelon giggled, his sneer even crueler than usual within the red light of his torch. "I see what you mean about your sister acting flighty. Ita—what was your name again?"

Without displaying a reaction to Gelon's seemingly deliberate confusion, Bek sawed through the bars until he had cut a hole into the grille big enough to walk through.

"I wonder why they put bars there in the first place," Itaweret said. "It's like there's something they wanted to cage inside it."

Gelon held his torch out into the blackness before them. "Of course there is. We call it treasure. Now stop bitching and go gather some with us!"

Standing alongside the tunnel walls were columns of stone that held up the earth like wooden frames propping up a mine shaft. Covering them were painted images of men and beasts, like those inside the cave. It reminded Itaweret of the painted temple column inscriptions in Per-Pehu, not to mention those inside the tombs of her people. Those were intended to depict and confer onto the Kemetian dead the afterlife they awaited. Had these prehistoric drawings served the same purpose for the Pelasgians of old?

If so, anything that lay inside this old tomb might have been meant for their usage in the next world. To take those belongings from them would be stealing from their spirits. If someone were to break into the tombs of her own people for the same purpose, Itaweret would cry out her outrage. What was different about what they planned to do here?

Then again, they needed silver to save her people. She could only pray the Pelasgians would understand.

The tunnel broadened until even the outlines of the walls retreated from the torch's illumination, leaving a lone isle of warm light in the cold black depths. There sounded only the soft tread of feet, the subtle crackle of dwindling flames, and Itaweret's own heavy breathing.

Far ahead, the staring faces of men and women seemed to float into the darkness. The torch fell from Gelon's hands as his girlish scream rang within the subterranean vault. Itaweret hugged onto her scepter with shivering arms.

Bek picked up the torch. He puffed a few breaths into the fire to rejuvenate it, revealing the faces once more. "No one need worry. They aren't alive."

The faces were all carved from slabs on top of marble boxes, each big enough to house a human body. These sarcophagi, or whatever the immense containers were, stood against the walls of the circular chamber surrounding them.

"It's like a crypt for a whole family," Itaweret said. "Or maybe a whole dynasty. Who would these people have been?"

Bek raised the torch to one of the faces, its eyes twinkling blue with inlaid sapphires. "Pelasgian chiefs, I presume. But . . . where is the treasure?"

"Maybe it's inside one of those things?" Gelon suggested. "Help me open that one!"

After handing Itaweret the torch, Bek and Gelon slipped their fingers under the giant lid. With sweat sparkling on their firelit skin, they heaved the slab aside with a unified groan, releasing a torrent of putrid rotten odor. It poured out from a skeletal body resting within the sarcophagus, with bits of flesh still clinging to bones and strands of grizzled hair hanging from the skull. Around the wrists, ankles, and neck gleamed jewelry of animal fangs, claws, and pieces of silver.

Bek clutched one of the necklaces with the laughter of relieved surprise. "So that's where this one was hiding his stash! Good thinking, Gelon. You think we should raid all of them?"

Gelon's grin stretched even wider. "Why not? Never mind a trip to Troy. Why, with a handful of this stuff, we'd be rich enough to buy our own army."

"Not so fast!" a reverberant voice growled. The language it spoke in was guttural and alien, yet for some unknown reason Itaweret was able to understand it as if it were her own native Kemetian.

A hand shot from the sarcophagus and grabbed Bek by the wrist, clenching him with fingers that grew flesh and skin out of their bones. The skeleton morphed into a tall man in a wolf-skin loincloth and silver jewelry, the brown skin over his corded muscles almost as dark as Itaweret and Bek's. His eyes smoldered with blue fire above his wicked thin-lipped snarl. "Steal from my people, and you shall face the wrath of our goddess!" the resurrected Pelasgian said.

His body disintegrated into dust and droplets of blood, trailed by the echo of cruel laughter.

Pulling his ears back and twitching his tail, Xiphos let out a low whine. Philos rose from the fallen megalith on which he had been sitting to give his lion a comforting rub behind the ears. "What's the matter, boy? You sense something?"

The ground trembled beneath his sandals. Several colossal stones shook as well, if the faint grating of rock against rock could be believed. Xiphos's mane spread out into a ball as Philos's own neck hairs stood on end.

Screams soon followed, each clearer than the last as the force— or whatever it was—escaped the mound's entrance. Beneath these cries of panic ran an undercurrent of what almost sounded like resonant cackling.

Was Athena behind this somehow?

Philos had not noticed the owl since they had left his village. The evil laughter—if laughter it was indeed—was too deep to be a woman's voice. If it wasn't her, then, who? Certainly, nothing mortal.

Itaweret, Bek, and Gelon ran from the mound. None of them seemed to be carrying any silver, as far as Philos could see. Itaweret wrapped her shuddering arms around Philos. "We've got to get out of here. Something is coming!"

"What on earth do you mean?" Philos asked.

"I don't know. It's some goddess of theirs. That is what the spirit in the tomb, or whatever it was, told us."

Again the earth shook, but with more violence than before. All around the ancient complex, stones fell and cracked into pieces, sending yet more tremors through the plateau's surface. One of these kicked Philos off his footing, rocking him over the turbulence like a branch among rapids.

The quaking escalated with an explosive roar alongside the rumble of ruptured soil.

Out of the mound's summit burst out a thick serpentine neck that reached up to the stars, glimmering with scales black as onyx. Its crocodile-like head, fringed with twisted horns, glared down with unblinking lava-orange eyes. The monstrous reptile opened its lance-tusked jaws big enough to swallow a whole cow and roared out a gust of boiling steam that stung Philos's skin.

He ducked and jumped toward Xiphos, who lay crouched while taunting the serpent with roars behind bared fangs. Retorting with an even louder cry that drowned out all other sound, the primeval deity dove after them, its maw agape. Philos could only cower beside his lion to get beneath the blasting force of the creature's fetid breath.

The monster's jaws did not close on them. Instead, the monster thrust its head back up to the sky, shrieking with blood and saliva flowing out of its mouth. One of its fangs rolled onto the grass at Itaweret's feet while she spun her red-stained scepter overhead.

The serpent lunged at her next. Itaweret escaped with a backward hop, and the beast's snout crashed into the earth with a spray of dirt and dust. Xiphos, roaring with renewed valor, pounced onto the side of its face and bit into the scaly hide. With one thrash of its skull, the reptile flung the lion off and then darted toward where he landed.

Philos jumped into its path and swatted its nostrils with his shepherd's staff. This time, the serpent did not recoil. It snapped at him until it clutched his tunic and craned him upward, his feet dangling in the air while he drummed his fists against the beast's jaws. Beneath him, the world shrank until his friends appeared tiny as ants and the megaliths mere pebbles.

"You can't have my friend like that, dragon!" Gelon yelled.

He chucked the torch into the reptile's neck. The monster let go, screeching in pain, and the world rushed back to Philos as he plummeted through the air. He closed his eyes, expecting to be smashed to pieces and sent to the underworld. There, at least, he could rejoin his father and the rest of his slaughtered people.

He landed not on hard earth, but soft muscular flesh. Bek and Itaweret had caught him in their arms. "Let's get out of here!" Bek said.

They raced to the edge of the plateau, leaving behind the monster and mound from which it had sprung. With a final roar, it sank back into the crater it had gouged, disappearing completely.

"At least that's over with," Philos said. "But where is the silver?"

Bek held the monster's splintered fang in his arms. "Maybe it will be ivory we pay them with. You have to admit, that'd be worth even more to them."

"Regardless, thank you and your sister for saving me there. And Gelon, too."

Gelon turned toward Itaweret with a sheepish smile. "I guess the Kemetian girl gets the most credit here. She's the one who got us the tooth to begin with."

"We couldn't have all gotten out of that without each other," Itaweret said. "Now, to Troy we go."

CHAPTER THIRTEEN

Sennuwy wriggled her feet over the dusty pavement to assuage their aching. She had spent the entire morning standing up, her oil-burnished shoulders rubbing against those of her compatriots within the crammed confines of the wooden cage they shared. Not even the dry noontime heat could beat away the chill that enveloped her figure, stripped naked with a slate placard hanging on a coarse rope around her neck.

The gawking and gossiping Mycenaean onlookers did nothing to warm her spirits. She would rather perish from starvation or thirst on the trek to get here, the way almost a third of her people had died, than put up with these barbarians' ogling.

A young Mycenaean ran up to the cage with a mischievous sneer. He reached past the cage's bars and planted his fingers into Sennuwy's backside. She could not slap him away, not with the manacles around her wrists. Nor could she shake him off with her hips without banging into one of the other captives. She could only endure his groping and lecherous laughter as he cracked an insulting joke about the "appetizing" dimensions of Kemetian women's rear ends.

Another Mycenaean spectator placed her hand on Sennuwy's hair and stroked it. "Feel how frizzy it is. It's almost like sheep's wool!"

"Don't you dare touch my hair, Achaean bitch!" Sennuwy snapped in her best Achaean.

The stout old slave dealer lashed his whip against the cage. "Silence, slave! You will not disrespect the free citizens of Mycenae."

"Oh, I wouldn't, if only they wouldn't disrespect *me!*"

She expected the dealer to strike again. Instead, he cracked a malevolent smile. "Then why don't we start today's auction early?"

He blew his bronze horn while hired guards pulled the cage door open. They barked orders for the Kemetians to trudge out in a single-file line, prodding them along with their spears. Not that anyone had a chance to break free. The captives' chains bound their manacles to one another so tightly that, even without the Mycenaeans' surveillance, escape was impossible.

Sennuwy walked at the front of the line. She stepped onto the stage of sunbaked marble that stood along the edge of Mycenae's *agora* opposite the shopkeepers' stalls. A thick arc of citizenry assembled before it. A burly Mycenaean in a white loincloth, body painted dark brown, beat a drum at the stage's far corner, hooting unintelligible lyrics that seemed to be a grotesque parody of Kemetian song.

The slave dealer marched to the drummer's side and blew his horn again. "Citizens of Mycenae, you know that our dear King Scylax has returned from his campaign against the Kemetian interlopers of Per-Pehu. I am honored to announce that he has entrusted none other than yours truly to distribute this little sampling of the fruits of his victory. Today, you too can come home with your very own lifelong Kemetian servant. May the highest bidders win!"

He strutted over to Sennuwy, grabbed her by her arms, and lifted her into the air. "Let us begin with our first specimen, a nubile young maiden by the name of Irene—"

"The name is Sennuwy!" she snarled.

The dealer tightened his grip on her arm, squeezing her muscles like a vise. "Your name shall be Irene henceforth! Now, as you can see, Irene here is quite an attractive sight, at least as far as these Kemetian wenches go. I hear she also has a lovely singing voice, not to mention some skill at dance and playing music. She'd make a great entertainer and cleaner for your household, not to mention your bed, for you gentlemen out there."

Male hands shot up from the ranks of the audience, clutching fat jiggling bags. They shouted out their prices in talents of gold, each higher than the last, the competing voices blending into a raucous din.

"Fifteen hundred, going once . . . twice . . . do I hear any other bids for this fine specimen?" the dealer asked. He waited a few seconds. "None? Then she's sold for fifteen hundred to the boy named Orion. Come up to inspect your purchase, you lucky young man!"

Sennuwy watched the winning bidder approach. He was the very same youth who had groped her earlier. He smacked and licked his lips as he walked onto the stage. After running his hands all over her body, Orion opened her mouth by pressing her chin down with his fingers. "Her teeth look even better than I expected," he said. "I thought these Kemetians all had their teeth worn down by gritty bread."

Sennuwy jerked her head away and then lunged and snapped her teeth at him.

Orion laughed, as did the crowd. "Ooh, I like them feisty like that! Here's your talents, good dealer. Now, why don't you come home with me so my friends and I can have our very first taste of dark meat?"

The instant the dealer had finished unlocking her manacles, Sennuwy leaped onto her buyer, pinning him down against the surface of the stage and hammering him with her liberated fists. "The only thing you'll taste is your own blood, you filthy Achaean jackal!"

With a thunderous crack, a sharp pain slashed across her back. The dealer pulled her by the hair off Orion and threw her off the stage, her blood dripping from the tip of his whip. Little fragments of stone on the road stabbed her skin after she landed. The dealer's guards loomed over her, a human ring constricting tighter and tighter.

"You will follow and obey your new master," one of them said. "Lest you find yourself thrown to our dogs!"

Sennuwy had exhausted the last of her will to resist her captors. She spent the last of her strength allowing Orion to help her up. Then, her legs gave way, and he dragged her through the crowd by the placard below her neck. She had perspired so much that her sweat washed away all the oil put on her body, but the chill that had haunted her earlier did not go away.

Instead, it grew worse—to the point where she became numb to almost all other feeling. Even the thumping of the painted drummer died away in Sennuwy's ears, replaced only by the throbbing of her own pulse. The cold, contemptuous sneers of the people she passed would have appalled even the cruelest demons in the under-world. As would the brutal drudgery that lay ahead of her, assum-ing she would be treated like any other slave. Sennuwy tried not to picture the things her new owner could do to her.

She noticed one Mycenaean face that did not reflect the cru-elty of the others. It was an old woman. Beneath her shawl, her eyes twinkled with sympathy as they met Sennuwy's. After the next blink, she was gone.

Scylax plopped down on his marble throne and rubbed his temples. With his conquest of Per-Pehu behind him, it was time to handle the less entertaining facets of ruling his nascent empire.

He stretched his legs over the glazed floor and ran his eyes along bright red, blue, and gold tiles that ran in alternating bands over the ceiling, glimmering from the glow of a circular hearth that lay between four scarlet columns in the center of the chamber. On the walls, painted lions, deer, and reclining griffins frolicked against a scenic background of wheat-yellow hills. He had spent so many years doing business in this room that his awe for the artwork had worn away, though it still possessed enough decorative charm to relax his temper.

He glanced at the second, smaller throne next to his own. Still empty. His queen should be there, her regal glamor reflected on his breastplate. Where was she? What was taking his damned older sister so long in capturing that Kemetian wench? A king could not properly rule without a queen to fill him with pride and produce his heir! Not only would the Kemetian be his queen, but also his slave, compelled to do anything he demanded.

Sandals clapped over the floor as the palace guards escorted in a stooping figure. They pulled her shawl down from her stringy white hair, revealing a leathery face with thin lips curled back, her teeth worn and crooked.

"So, you are the old crone named Malthake?" Scylax said. "Why couldn't you get your husband to speak for you?"

"He has been no more, descended to the realm of Hades, for twenty years now," Malthake said. "But I don't need any man to speak my mind. Not even against you."

"Let me guess, you're here to call me a tyrant and a warmonger. How inventive."

"Not only that. I know you do not bother yourself with what goes down at the marketplace, but the slave auction today was even more appalling than usual. I saw a young woman degraded, whipped, and then thrown away to be violated by her purchaser and his friends. I don't even want to imagine what the rest went through!"

Scylax rolled his eyes. "It's a slave auction. What do you expect? And besides, they were all Kemetians this time."

"Why does it matter? They are human beings like you and me. Their skin, hair, and way of life may be different from ours, but not their souls."

"Hold on, how do you know that? You already know that Kemetians are different from us on the outside. Why assume they are the same as us within?"

"Why assume otherwise?"

Scylax got off his throne and walked to one of the depictions of deer on the walls. "You know that a deer or a lion is not like us in soul as well as body. They not only look different, but they act and think unlike us as well. Now, something like a monkey or an ape might be closer to us in intelligence and personality as well as appearance, but you know they are still not *quite* like us."

"But those are all wild animals. We're talking about human beings of a different color."

"Oh, so you believe the differences are only skin deep, Malthake? How do you know that? What makes you so sure that the creatures we call human beings are all the same in spirit or aptitude, regardless of whence they came? You know that some men and women are smarter, wiser, and nobler than others. Could not the same be said of nations compared to one another?"

"My king, with all due respect, *you* are the one assuming they must be different. And even if that were so, does that mean we can treat people of other races however we want? Why, most treat their dogs better than how I saw that poor young woman treated!"

"Well, I'm not in charge of how every one of my citizens treats their slaves. I will say, though, that your sympathy toward those Kemetians is undeserved. Do you not recall, old woman, that the colonists of Per-Pehu made war with the Achaean villages nearby and enslaved them too? Why should we, as Achaeans, feel bad for the Kemetians receiving the treatment they were all too happy to deliver themselves?"

"Because we should be better than that!"

Scylax laughed. "Better than them, you say? So much for your insistence that the Kemetians are our equals. Listen, I have a city to rule and an empire to forge. There's enough on my hands without having to entertain a soft-hearted old crone like you. Begone!"

Malthake stood in place, her arms crossed. "Not until you stop and recant your cruelty. If you were at least half the king your elder brother was—"

"Silence!"

In the next moment, the old woman's head rolled off her neck with a red-washed sweep of Scylax's sword and bounced onto the floor. Even the guards stood trembling with widened eyes.

Scylax tapped the disembodied head with his sandal. "Have this mounted on the palace gates as a warning. Once and for all, the people of Mycenae must learn that nobody, Achaean or anyone else, challenges their king or questions my decisions. No one."

CHAPTER FOURTEEN

A jetty of stone rubble paved over with earth projected into the river from its reedy eastern bank. The water slowed and spread into a marshy delta clouded with thick mist and swarms of buzzing insects. From behind the fog alongside the jetty emerged a deep violet, rectangular sail billowing with a bull's head outlined in white.

While swatting a mosquito from her cheek, Itaweret said her thanks to Mut and the gods of Kemet for her good fortune.

A couple of days had drifted past since they had left behind the plateau with the Pelasgian tomb and megaliths. Together, Bek and Gelon hauled the giant serpent's fang on their shoulders. It would have been a dull journey had the bugs and the mud sticking onto her feet and the edges of her linen gown not persisted in tormenting her. If she had anything kind to say about this miserable stretch of swampland, it was that they had not seen anything like the predatory crocodiles or ill-tempered hippopotamuses that haunted the Nile Delta back in Kemet.

On the bank behind the jetty, a camp sprouted up of goat-hair tents dyed purple like the ship's sail. Men in sweat-stained tunics squatted around campfires and talked in coarse Phoenician. The sailors were all bronze-skinned, intermediate between Achaeans and most Kemetians in color, with thick black beards and hairy forelimbs and shins. As Itaweret led her party into the encampment, the sailors smelled like they had not bathed in weeks.

One of the Phoenicians whistled toward her. "What do you think you're doing here, woman?" the sailor called out. "You going to trade that big tusk your friends are carrying?"

"Since when were there elephants in Achaea, anyway?" another Phoenician muttered. "I'd be mighty suspicious if I were you."

"I assure you, we're carrying genuine ivory," Itaweret said. "You can come over and feel it for yourselves."

Yet another sailor grinned as he bounced his eyebrows. "Why don't we touch your, ahem, anatomy while we're at it, pretty one?"

A slim, dark shadow whizzed a finger's span over his scalp, lodging deep into the trunk of a nearby tree. The soldier fell onto his knees in a groveling pose, whimpering like a frightened little boy.

It was a woman who had shot that arrow with her bow. Her ebony skin was even darker than Itaweret's own, her tall and lean figure clad with a short scarlet loincloth and top as well as a necklace of green malachite beads. The Phoenicians stopped their chatter and watched with deference as she approached Itaweret.

"Sorry for the rude greeting you've received," the archer woman said. "Men like these will pounce on any young woman that catches their fancy. It's why I always keep my bow and quiver with me."

"Is she Kemetian, too?" Philos asked.

Bek shook his head. "She's from Wawat, right upriver of Kemet. I'd recognize one of those bright-red loincloths anywhere."

Itaweret remembered from her studies that, for a long time, the people of Wawat and Kemet did not get along at all. At one point, the Kemetians even conquered Wawat in a series of bloody and devastating wars, all in the name of border security and controlling trade along the Nile. Why was this woman not showing any sign of a grudge against her Kemetian visitors after all the past bloodshed?

"Call me Nebta, Captain of the *Bull of Heaven*," the Wawatian said. "I've been with these Phoenicians for ten years now. They were kind enough to give me a home aboard after the Kushites came in and sacked my hometown."

"Wait a moment, who are these Kushites?" Philos asked. "Are they also south of Kemet?"

"Correct, they're further up the Nile from us. Think of my people as being wedged between Kemet in the north and Kush in the south. And we've suffered for centuries because of that."

"Then why did you help me, Nebta?" Itaweret said. "Don't you think we Kemetians have much to answer for as well?"

"Your pharaohs might. But you can't help where you were born or how your king behaves, and I'd rather not have one of my men mishandle a woman—no matter where she comes from." She looked at Bek and Gelon. "Where'd you get that big tusk?"

Gelon laid the serpent's fang at Nebta's feet. "It's a long and incredible story, believe me. We didn't get it from an elephant, or whatever you call it. My associates were hoping you'd do them a little favor in return for it."

"We want to go to Troy," Bek added. "Would it be too much of a detour for you to bring us there?"

Nebta picked up the huge fang in her arms. "Even if it's not from an elephant, it seems to be real ivory. And it *would* make us a killing at the next market . . . but what business would you have at Troy?"

"Have you not heard? The Mycenaeans sacked Per-Pehu, our home, almost a week ago," Itaweret said. "They've taken the rest of our people in chains. We want to liberate them, and we need the Trojans' help to do so."

"You mean to drag us into this conflict, don't you?" one of the Phoenician sailors asked, his voice dripping with resentment.

Nebta looked around her camp, her men watching. "As someone who had her own home destroyed in war, I know better than most why you want to do this," she said. "And in truth, I would be more than happy to aid your quest. The problem is that I don't want my men to get caught in this crossfire between you and the Mycenaeans. If they find out we've assisted you—"

"All that means is that we should leave as soon as possible," Philos said. "We know one of their spies is hunting us down, and trust me when I say that none of these sailors would be a match for the soldiers she's bringing along. They've already wiped out my own village, in addition to Per-Pehu."

"Really? Then you are right. We'll set sail tomorrow morning at latest. And you are all welcome to come aboard. Even your, um, pet over there."

Philos chuckled as he petted his lion. "Oh, Xiphos here? I've raised him since he was a cub. He won't bite unless you piss him off."

"Hope you all have a safe voyage," Gelon said. "As for me, I'd rather stay here. There are plenty of other villages here in Achaea I can move into."

Philos turned to his friend with a nod. "I do think it's a shame you don't want to come along, but it's up to you. May Zeus and all the other gods watch over you. And please keep an eye out for those Mycenaeans."

After a final wave of his hand, Gelon turned and walked away from the encampment until the swamp's mist shrouded his entire form.

"Good riddance to him," Bek muttered.

Itaweret bumped her brother's arm with her elbow. "Bek! Show some respect."

"Like he showed much respect to us . . ."

"That'll be enough bickering for the day, you two," Nebta said. "Why don't you all follow me to my tent. I'll be more than happy to accommodate you personally over the night before we leave."

Day receded into dusk as Gelon advanced north through the marshland, wishing he'd elected to join his friend and the others on their journey. It would mean spending yet more weeks beside those two Kemetians, but even their company would be preferable to none. Plus, in truth, they had done nothing to hurt him throughout their time together. All Gelon ever had to justify his distaste for them was how other Kemetians had treated his people in the past. Was that good reason to mistreat the harmless pair?

You cannot help where you were born. The woman from Wawat had said that to the Kemetian girl. If she did not begrudge the Kemetians for how their ancestors had behaved toward her own people, perhaps he might have shown them the same courtesy.

Now, he had no one to protect him from the surrounding wilds but himself. Not even Philos and his lion would be there to keep watch through the night. Without them, Gelon could very well find himself devoured by wolves or other predators before the next sunrise. He could blame nothing but his decision for that fate.

He heard the hoot of an owl.

Overhead, the bird perched on the naked branch of a dead tree and looked at him with a pair of luminous silver-gray eyes he'd thought he had seen before. Was that the owl—

"Don't you look familiar?"

The Mycenaean woman with the wolf-skin shawl stood in front of Gelon, her armored soldiers blocking the path through the marsh. Gelon knelt before the Mycenaeans, quivering like a child confronted by angry parents. "I mean you no harm, mistress. Please, let me through."

"Ah, yes, you're from the same village as the son of Metrophanes, aren't you?" the woman asked. "You weren't helping them escape, were you?"

"No, I had nothing to do with that."

The owl hooted again. The woman nodded at the bird and then slapped Gelon, her nails cutting bloody scars across his cheeks. "Don't lie to me, villager! Tell me where your friend and his Kemetian associates went. You know what will happen if you don't!"

Her soldiers drew their spears and thrust them toward the cowering Gelon. He would have no chance against them. If that owl had the power to see through his lies, he had no hope of misleading them, either.

Gelon's voice melted into a whimper. "They went to Troy, my lady. They should be setting sail tomorrow, if not tonight. How are you going to catch them? You couldn't exactly swim after them, could you?"

The woman in the wolf-skin shawl smiled. "I don't need to. I know an even better way. Speaking of which, my owl is a little hungry. I must say, she's rather partial to sacrificial human flesh."

"Whatever you're thinking, my lady, don't! I've been through enough trouble already. Please, have mercy . . ."

The woman nodded to one of her soldiers, who drew his sword and ran the blade's ice-cold edge across the skin of Gelon's neck. His painful yelp turned to gagging as the sword sawed through his gullet. With another chopping motion of the weapon, his world turned black and numb forever.

CHAPTER FIFTEEN

Itaweret slumped over the gunwale alongside the *Bull of Heaven*'s starboard side, resting her arms on the wooden railing and yawning.

When they first launched from the jetty into the open sea, she was thrilled by the cool marine breeze blowing past her and stroking her hair. The force of the wind, combined with the tireless rowing of the Phoenician oarsmen to the rhythm of the drivers' drumming, had allowed the broad-sterned galley to zip over the water with incredible speed, the adjacent coastline blending into a blur of greens and browns over the wine-dark water.

Though less than half a week had passed since that initial burst of speed, the excitement had subsided beneath monotony. Itaweret had looked forward to spending the rest of her voyage aboard a vessel where she would stand safe from predators and other perils of the wilderness. She never expected to *miss* that part of the adventure, as she did in a weird way now. Even the exhaustion of hiking through rugged terrain kept her more occupied than idling for hours upon hours on a rocking deck.

A school of darting fish shimmered just beneath the surface, beside the ship's hull. So far, Itaweret had seen nothing more impressive than those tiny creatures. She had hoped to catch a glimpse of the more magnificent beasts claimed by the sailors to dwell within the depths. Prowling sharks, leaping dolphins, gargantuan whales that spouted jets of water from nostrils above their eyes. Even the humongous squids said to be capable of dragging down boats with their tentacles would be better than nothing.

Nebta leaned against the deckhouse on the center of the galley's stern, whistling a tune while sharpening the arrows in her quiver with a whetstone. Next to the Wawatian stood Bek, who stared at her with an eager smile, not unlike the one Itaweret had received from Philos several times.

Nebta glanced sideways at her admirer. "Are you checking me out?"

"Um . . . no," Bek said. "I was, uh, observing your sharpening techniques."

She shook her head with a disbelieving smirk. "Sure you were. That's why you were paying particular attention to my chest and behind."

Itaweret tried to stifle a laugh. "Girl, do I know how you feel."

"Not that I blame him," Philos added. "You two are both, shall I say—"

Itaweret shook her head, the smile leaving her face. "Good gods, is ogling women everything on your mind? You're like starved jackals eying pieces of meat!"

"Calm down, my Kemetian sister," Nebta said. "Men are always going to appreciate women like you and me. You might as well use it to your advantage. Besides, it's not like we women are necessarily any better around handsome men."

Itaweret shook her head with a grumble of frustration. "Fair enough. But you can't deny that having to put up with it all the time grows tiresome."

She stormed away to the opposite side of the galley, positioning herself at the far corner of the stern where nobody else could see her. Twice she looked back, at once surprised and relieved that none of the men had tried to follow her. Hopefully, she'd made her point—she did not want any of them gawking in her direction.

Perhaps Itaweret should have forgiven them. It was natural for men to investigate women they found attractive. Still, the man who could learn to not bother her with his gaze would be showing her the most basic form of respect.

Behind the ship, a pair of silver sparks flashed above the sea on the horizon. They appeared embedded within a long, narrow silhouette that grew with every flap of its feathered wings.

Itaweret looked up. That damned owl of Kleno's!

As it advanced toward them, it expanded in size until it was at least big enough to carry off an ox. Once it had soared over the gunwale's lip, the overgrown bird reared up and extended its

talons, now longer than sabers, toward Itaweret. The aching, resonant shrillness of its cry overpowered her senses, forcing her onto
her knees, the claws drawing nearer.

The twang of a bowstring followed, and then the swift, wet
noise of metal puncturing flesh. The monstrous owl faltered backward, an arrow embedded in its breast, soiling the white plumage
with a spreading red stain. As the owl thrashed its wings in a desperate effort to keep itself in mid-air, Nebta bombarded it with a
succession of shots.

The bird shrieked once more as it dove after the Wawatian,
crashing into her and pinning her down with its talons while stabbing at her with its beak. Itaweret pounced on its back and wrapped
her arms around its neck to restrain its head from Nebta. It took
one bucking motion for the giant avian to throw her off.

Landing with a roll over the deck, Itaweret then sprang toward
the galley's deckhouse in search of shelter. Before she could get
there, the owl's talons clenched onto her arms, squeezing her flesh
to the bone. Her heels dragged backward over the wooden planks
as she rattled her limbs against the pressure of the bird's pulling
grasp.

Finally, it dropped her.

Xiphos seized the owl's tail feathers in his fangs, yanking it away
from Itaweret while Philos battered its head with his staff. Some of
the Phoenician sailors rushed from their rowers' benches to further
torture the creature with pricks and jabs from their scimitars.

Bek tossed his dagger to Itaweret. "I'll give you the honor of
finishing it off."

She whirled around and hurled the dagger into the bloodied
bird's eye.

It did not die. Instead, it exploded into a ball of silver light that
swept across the galley, throwing everyone off their feet. When the
light cleared, all that remained was a stream of cloudy smoke flowing back to the heavens, then dissipating.

"Whoa! Does that mean we killed it?" Nebta asked.

"I don't know," Itaweret replied. "I have no idea whether mortals like ourselves could kill that sort of thing. We can only hope it
doesn't show up again."

"Even if it does, it'll probably be a while," Philos said. "By the way, that was one mean throw of yours, Itaweret. It almost makes me jealous."

Itaweret raised an eyebrow and smirked. "*Almost*, you say?"

"Well . . . uh . . . It doesn't matter. The point is, it was a good throw."

"Thank you, anyway."

Kleno screamed the foulest curse imaginable into the heavens. Flocks of frightened birds fled squawking from the treetops and the reeds of the marsh beside the abandoned pier on which the priestess of Mycenae stood. She never would have thought it possible. Athena, the goddess she had served her whole life, had failed her. Not only that, but that Kemetian wench, that dark-hued mortal, had somehow managed to slay her incarnation.

Of course, no mortal could kill divinity for good. Only other gods could do that. Still, slaying a god's fleshy incarnation on earth was no minor blow. It might be days, weeks, or even years before Athena could recover from such an injury.

There was no use in pursuing the Kemetian girl further. She had wasted enough time on the chase, and her little brother was never the most patient man. It was time to come home.

Still, there remained a sliver of hope. If the Kemetians and their helpers were bound for Troy, all anyone had to do to track them down was meet them at a spot along the way. Scylax would be more than happy to attack.

Kleno turned around from the tip of the jetty and walked back to where her retinue of soldiers stood. "I think I know where our king should launch his next campaign."

CHAPTER SIXTEEN

Something—or someone—tapped twice on the reed door from outside, rattling the stems each time.

Goosebumps rose on Sennuwy's arms. More than tiredness after the day's work kept her lying down on her sleeping bench. Whenever anyone knocked on her cramped slave-hut's door this late after sundown, she knew they came with more than simple household chores to assign her. Menial as they were, at least chores did not cause her nearly as much pain and abuse. Pain lingered between her legs to the point where she could barely walk in a straight line.

More raps on the door. "Irene! What is taking you so damned long?" It was Orion.

She refused to get up. "Leave me to rest tonight, master. I am . . . very worn out. Go bother one of the others."

With one crackling punch, the door fell and splintered. Orion's countenance, contorted by growling fury, glowed like a demon from the oil lamp he carried. "Don't you dare talk back to me, slave!" the Mycenaean youth said. "How many times must I tell you that?"

"As many times until you give up and leave me alone!"

Orion's hand pounded across her cheek like a bludgeon. Grabbing her by the hair, the roots barely staying within the skin of her scalp, he dragged her out through the doorway onto the dusty alley between her hut and his family's manor. The squirming Sennuwy flailed her arms until she seized hold of her owner's arm and punctured his skin with her fingernails. After Orion let go with a girlish yelp, she spun herself on one leg and kicked in his nose with her other heel.

"You damned Kemetian bitch!" Orion gurgled in a voice turned nasally. "I'll have you put to death for that!"

Sennuwy cackled. "Do it, then—before I do you in first!"

Doors banged open from the row of neighboring slave-huts. All the other enslaved Kemetians on Orion's estate charged out to join Sennuwy in pouncing on their owner, raining their fists and feet down in a downpour every bit as ruthless as the abuse they had suffered themselves.

"Stop! What's going on here?"

The vengeful Kemetians withdrew their pounding fists the moment they heard the voice. A pair of Mycenaean town guardsmen, armored up and armed with spears, broke through the estate's front gate and marched into the scene.

Sennuwy pointed to the crumpled, bruised Orion at her feet. "We've endured enough of his abuses and violations," she said. "Is rebelling not within our rights?"

"Within your *rights*?" The foremost of the guards laughed. "For Zeus's sake, woman, you're *his* property. He can do whatever he likes to you!"

"That doesn't mean we will put up with it. Now you leave us be, or he dies!"

Orion raised his twitching arm up. "H-how ab-bout I m-make you an of-fer? I'll f-free you all if y-you l-let me liv-live . . ."

Sennuwy shook her head. "Am I supposed to trust you now? How do I know you won't simply have your men round up us again?"

The bruise-mottled Achaean youth said nothing as he lifted a hand to scratch his hair.

"You know what, I'll accept on one condition," Sennuwy continued. "I want your guards to witness you saying you'll free us, or we'll kill you right now."

Orion gave her a weak nod. "F-fair e-enough."

Scylax pulled out the largest scroll of papyrus from its niche in the wall of his private study. He unfolded the scroll on his desk, cautious not to crinkle it to the point of tearing, and hovered it over a miniature oil lamp held with his finger. The lamp was the sole source of illumination within the room, since dawn was still untucking itself from the night.

Mycenaean tradition had always attributed authorship of the map to Perseus, the son of Zeus who had founded the city back in the heroic ages. Whatever the truth behind that specific claim, Scylax could never disagree that the weathered and smudged papyrus had passed from generations of kings to their sons. Its wear had changed little since he had teased his brother by trying to peek at it over the latter's shoulder during their boyhoods.

Scylax could not resist a nostalgic smile. With Metrophanes removed from the scene, the new king of Mycenae could pour over the map all by himself, and for as long as he wanted.

This was no crude sketch of continental contours outlined in black ink with an uneven hand, like one might buy from a common mapmaker's stall in the agora. The original cartographer had taken great care in decorating the terrain with ranges of jagged brown mountains, green forests and tufts of grass, and rolling expanses of yellow dunes. Cities appeared not as simple dots or squares, but as tiny representations of their native architecture, be they Babylonian ziggurats, tapered Kemetian temples, or walled Achaean cities like Mycenae itself. Even the oceans churned with deep-blue waves with dolphins, octopuses, and whales swimming beside sailing ships, much as wild animals were drawn roaming the land.

There were also depictions of humanity across the world. Every country represented on the map had at least one human being showing how the inhabitants of that country looked and dressed. Toward the upper edge of the map, cut off from Achaea by mountains, lived the warlike tribes of white men with yellow hair and swirling blue tattoos, with fur capes over their woolen tunics. By contrast, those that occupied the map's bottom half were colored deep brown to pure black, needing only loincloths of white linen for the hot climates they inhabited. Toward the right lived various groups of tawny to pale yellow-brown people, with some of the latter having eyes drawn so narrow they might as well be slits. And in the areas within the map's center, such as Achaea itself, were men of Scylax's own color, armored with bronze, the true warriors they were.

They would show the world how to fight. With Per-Pehu now in ashes, its citizens under his Mycenaean yoke, all Scylax needed to do was find where to bring his champions next.

A couple of soft bumps on the study door. A woman's voice whistled through its planks.

Scylax grumbled as he turned away to open the door. He grew silent, halting where he stood, when he recognized the gleam of his sister's eyes. "Kleno? You've come back at last?"

Kleno pulled the mud- and blood-splattered shawl off her shoulders and held her head low. "I couldn't keep you waiting forever, little brother. Though I must apologize for the disappointing resolution. That Kemetian girl was more . . . slippery than we anticipated."

Scylax balled his hands into fists. "All the gods be damned!" He snarled like a provoked dog. "Damn, damn them all! I should have figured you'd let her get away. And what of your owl?"

"She . . . got that too. But believe me, Brother, I bring good news as well. I know where Itaweret and her allies are headed. And, as an aside, I even found out what really happened to our brother all those years ago."

Scylax's jaw dropped. His fists trembled as he wrestled to restrain himself from punching his sister's teeth out. "You mean the bandits you hired hadn't disposed of him like you said? Were you lying to me this whole time, woman?"

"Trust me, it would be more accurate to say he escaped our first attempt instead. I don't know how. We found him in a village not far from Per-Pehu, with a wife and son of his own. Thankfully, we were able to correct our original mistake. I saw his death with my own eyes this time."

"I suppose that's better than never killing him. You say he had a son? How old?"

"Early twenties, I would guess. A boy named Philos. He's been helping Itaweret since our initial encounter. Together, they're headed for Troy."

Scylax furrowed his brow, then a smile stretched almost the width of his face. Muffled laughter emerged from behind his teeth. "Troy, you say? That would be quite the fitting refuge if I do say so myself. We all know their current regime has the most welcoming attitude toward settlers from afar, don't we, big sister?"

"That is a good point," Kleno said. "Nonetheless, if there is the off chance that he really will give them asylum, I say they'd make a fine target for your next campaign. That is, if you can't get their king to turn them in."

"Oh, that shouldn't be too hard. But, if push must come to shove, I wouldn't mind a more entertaining challenge for my men. Those half-naked Kemetian defenders would have been anticlimactic opponents. Still, I must ask one more thing—when are you going to get a new owl?"

Kleno patted her shoulder where Athena had once perched. "In normal circumstances, gods take anywhere between a few days and weeks to regenerate their earthly incarnations. But you know, Brother, there *is* a way for us mortal priests to accelerate the process. All it takes is a little . . . sacrifice."

"What should we sacrifice, then?"

"What else? Human flesh. It does the trick nicely."

"That shouldn't be too hard. I can even picture what kind of recent troublemakers will come in handy for that."

Together, he and Kleno cackled together with eager glee.

CHAPTER SEVENTEEN

❝ I see land!"

From the crow's nest atop the *Bull of Heaven*'s mast, one of the younger Phoenician sailors cried out his welcome observation, again and again.

Itaweret jogged out of the deckhouse to the galley's portside gunwale. Nearly a week had gone by since they had sailed out of view of the coastline, with only open ocean surrounding the ship. Ever since that point, she had found herself forced to sleep within the deckhouse while the boat continued to rise, fall, and sway over the waves, instead of being anchored beside the beach for the night. Even if she looked past the lack of comfortable cushioning in her bunk, Itaweret could not ignore how all that constant motion had shaken her stomach with chronic nausea.

As the drivers slapped their drums with a renewal of frenetic energy, the morning mist that floated over the sea cleared away, exposing the irregular outline of rocky hills studded with trees and flat-roofed buildings. Standing on the highest summit were crenelated ramparts of alabaster-pale mudbrick on a foundation of rubble, with giant gold-leaved frescoes showing horses—what the Achaeans called those zebras with no stripes—galloping over the walls' outward face.

"Welcome to Troy, my Kemetian friend," Nebta said. "Hope you enjoyed our little trip together."

"You're not coming along?" Itaweret asked.

"Sorry, but no. Remember, our agreement said I would bring you here. I'm the captain of traveling merchants, so I've plenty of places to go after this."

"It's simply that, after seeing my brother hang around you so often the past few days, I would have thought . . . you know . . ."

Nebta rolled her eyes with a groan. "Tell him I'm sorry to disappoint him. If he really wants to . . . spend more time with me like *that*, he'll have to stay with me instead of going with you. Is that what either of you want?"

"Aw, come on, you could use a break from sailing." Bek stepped from behind the women. "Not to mention, we could use archery skills like those you showed against that big Mycenaean owl."

"Why would you need my archery skills after that? You weren't planning to *attack* the Trojans the whole time, were you?"

"No, but who knows what lies ahead of us next?" Itaweret said. "We may have slain the owl, but that doesn't mean Scylax won't have other spies lurking around."

Nebta shifted her gaze to where Xiphos the lion slept, curled up right within the deck's hind quarter. "With that big a pet following you, I don't think you would need my aid any further."

"And how do you know that?" Bek said. "You have the best range out of any of us. Even my knife throwing isn't *that* good! C'mon, girl, we would benefit from your company."

"You mean, *you* would benefit from my company. Or at least desire it." Nebta winked with a cheeky smile. "Not that I mind it that much, my handsome companion."

Philos whistled and pointed toward the nearing shore. On the wooden pier that projected from the beach, a troop of twenty spearmen marched, their bronze armor and equipment recalling that of the Mycenaeans. There was one difference: the crests streaming from their helmets were deep blue instead of red.

After the galley slipped by the dock and its stone anchor plopped into the water, the leading soldier crossed his arms next to where the gangplank was laid, his brow furrowed with suspicion. Tall and muscular in build, he glowed with the olive skin of an Achaean and wore a thick black beard with faint white striping.

"I hope we're not in trouble already," Philos said.

Philos scurried down to the pier and nodded before the soldiers' captain. "What's the matter, sir? We are humble travelers, brought here by merchants. We mean you no harm."

"I've no reason to doubt that yet, young man," the other spoke with an accent slightly more nasal than a typical Achaean's. "It's a matter of precaution prompted by recent developments."

"What on earth do you mean?" Itaweret asked.

The Trojan captain hesitated for a moment, then asked, "Are any of your lot planning to stay in Troy hereon?"

"Not for very long, sir," Bek said. "We only seek a brief audience with your king."

"Praised be Poseidon, then. The problem, you see, is that we've had a bit of a, um, *foreigner* crisis of late. Hundreds upon hundreds have been coming from all over the world to settle within our borders. See for yourself on those hills!"

Itaweret took a closer look at the slopes descending toward the sea from Troy's walls. Almost all the space between the rocky outcroppings and cedar trees was covered with a dense clutter of crude and disheveled tents, huts, and hovels obscured by a fog of campfire smoke. She could smell the smoke, along with much less pleasant odors, from the dock.

Was this where Troy housed her refugees? It didn't look like a place anyone in the world, no matter how desperate, would want to live. Even the quaint, primitive huts of Taurocephalus were more inviting than the overgrown slum. The poor people!

"What brought them all here?" Itaweret asked.

"It started with refugees from the countryside to our east, fleeing the Hittites a little over twenty years ago. Since then, they've been coming from all directions and all continents. Minoans, Achaeans, Mitanni, Babylonians, even Kemetians like yourself—all kinds of people. It's like the entire world sees Troy as this all-accepting sanctuary where anybody can move in and leech from our granaries!"

Philos furrowed his brow. "Excuse me, *leech*? Is that how you speak of—"

"That's enough, everyone," Nebta said. "Sir, would you and your men be kind enough to escort us to your king? We need an audience with him. It's quite important."

The Trojan captain saluted her. "We would be more than happy. No, it'd be our duty. The road between here and the city does run uncomfortably close to all those shacks you saw. For your own safety, I'd advise against falling too far behind."

He led his soldiers marching toward the end of the dock, with Itaweret and her companions huddling close behind them.

Philos leaned over to mutter into the priestess's ear. "I don't think this will end as well as it should."

CHAPTER EIGHTEEN

Even from a distance, the ramshackle village outside of Troy was an unpleasant eyesore, Itaweret thought. As the road leading from the docks veered closer to a border fence of sharpened stakes, the sight of affairs in the settlement stung her eyes to the point of tearing. Not only due to the opaque mist of smoke that floated over it.

Men and women of all ages and colors hugged close to one another, clogging the crevices that passed for streets and alleyways between their assorted shelters. As diverse as their origins were, the migrants all shared a tendency toward emaciated figures underneath soiled clothing, with even the smallest children slowly turning into skeletons clothed tight with skin. One mother, as dark-complexioned as Itaweret herself, whimpered an uncertain lullaby to the toddler boy and girl she embraced with her scarred, bony arms.

Itaweret could not quite make out the lyrics of the mother's song, but she recognized the language as Kemetian. Its melody reminded her of a song her own mother would sing to her before bed when she was a little girl. Her eyes turned wet with memories of her devastated home, its gardens and columns and whitewashed walls decorated with murals and hieroglyphs. She could never return to it, much as this woman—a refugee like herself—would never return to her home.

From the other side of the fence, people screamed and yelled while oncoming soldiers stamped their feet. Migrants tumbled aside or flew into the air after Trojan soldiers kicked and slapped their way through the shivering masses with the force of barreling rhinos. They stopped the moment they reached the black woman with the two kids and formed a semicircle, trapping her in front of her crumbling hut. Without a word or the briefest hesitation, the soldiers proceeded to rip both son and daughter out of their mother's arms.

Philos bared his teeth in a darkened and contorted face. "What in Hades's name is going on over there?"

"It's our policy," the captain said. "Sorry, but it's the best deterrent we have for some of these foreigners, lest more of them come to pile up beside our walls."

"Tearing kids away from their mothers is a deterrent? Monstrous! You're almost as bad as Scylax of Mycenae himself!"

"Don't worry, the children will be safe in captivity—"

Summoning Xiphos with a whistle, Philos and his lion sprang over the fence together, hurtling to where the mother struggled to reclaim her children. A battle of shepherd's staff and feline claws against Trojan bronze broke out the moment they collided.

"Philos, *no!*" Itaweret screamed. "We've got to go after him!"

"You think you can talk him back to his senses?" Bek asked. "Because you don't have much time left!"

"Then I'll be off!"

With the aid of Mut's scepter, Itaweret vaulted over the fence and landed where Philos and his lion were engaging the soldiers. Two of the Trojans had already gone down, with one sporting a dark-purple stain on his brow. The other wore a gory mess where eyes, nose, cheeks, mouth, and jaw once sat before the lion mauled it off. The mother and her children were gone, having fled the carnage.

"Stop it, Philos!" Itaweret yelled over the clangor. "This is nothing but madness!"

"This is justice!" Philos said.

He smacked away another Trojan with a blow to the back of the head. Xiphos seized the staggering soldier's neck with his fangs before the Trojan had finished falling.

Itaweret grabbed Philos by the shoulder, dug her nails into his skin, and pulled him away. "Listen, I know how you feel—believe me, what those men were doing was wrong. But getting into trouble with Trojan law is the last thing we need at this very moment!"

"You, Kemetian girl!" It was one of the Trojans who remained standing. "Is the young Achaean an accomplice of yours?"

"An *associate*, yes," Itaweret said. "But I don't endorse how he assaulted you and your colleagues. Come, Philos and Xiphos. We can settle this with their king later."

After kicking out an opening through the fence, the Trojan captain marched in, followed by Bek and Nebta. He crossed his arms and nodded. "As you should. Though you should all pray that our King Aleksandros is in a much more temperate and under-standing mood than usual."

"Whatever his mood, he has a *lot* to answer for," Philos said. "Itaweret, priestess of Per-Pehu, do you really want to have any-thing to do with him now?"

Philos had a point. Any king who would seize the children of desperate refugees—for any reason—would never make a sympa-thetic ally, even if they were able to talk him into helping foreign-ers. In truth, Itaweret thought, if he was willing to mistreat people in order to protect what he considered his belongings, he might be as terrible as Scylax himself.

"We can deal with his immigration policies after we've resolved everything else," Bek said. "What we need now is all the help we can get."

Itaweret looked back at the bruised and mauled soldiers. The mother and her children peeked from behind the trunk of a deceased cedar tree further down the street, between the tents and huts. Their eyes met hers, and they nodded without saying a single word.

"May the gods protect you and your family," Itaweret said under her breath.

CHAPTER NINETEEN

A chill more severe than winter shivered throughout Philos's body, turning his sweat-soaked body cold. Never in his entire life had he encountered a man-made structure which rose as close to the heavens as this gatehouse to Troy, a titanic construction of mud bricks laid upon stone. Nor had he seen wooden doors like those locked within its one gaping opening. Not even the megaliths erected by the bygone Pelasgians could silence the shepherd boy with such awe—and dread.

Bek rubbed his arm across Philos's shoulder with a teasing snicker. "You think that's wondrous to behold? You should have seen the one we had at Per-Pehu! For starters, it was even taller—"

Itaweret flashed a scolding glare at her brother. "Don't make it worse for him!"

"Considering what your Achaean friend has already got us into, I don't think he has much lower to sink," Nebta said.

Philos took two steps backward from the Wawatian woman. He rested his leg against Xiphos's flank and patted the panting lion's mane. In a world fractured and plagued by the cruelty of humanity toward their own, the company of even the fiercest wild predator had become preferable. At least lions and other animals of the plain had no way of speaking the words that could wound a man's spirit. Also, as long as you trained them with enough care, you could trust their loyalty far more.

The doors to Troy parted with a creaking groan, like the yawn of a colossal monster eager to engulf everyone in a single inhalation. Terrifying as the thought was, it was far more desirable to what awaited Philos and his companions now. At least their deaths would come quick and with only the briefest shot of pain.

The captain of the Trojan escort strutted back to where Philos stood and prodded him with the hilt of his sword. "What are you waiting for? Keep up!"

Xiphos parted his lips with a low growl at the Trojan officer, but Philos tapped his head while whispering calming words. Both he and the lion had delivered, and received, enough punishment for the day. Following their hosts' orders was their sole remaining option.

The shepherd of Taurocephalus had expected Troy to overwhelm him ever since he had first noticed the contours of its famous walls, its massive scale. Even that became an underestimation the very moment he and his allies entered, with its gate clapping shut behind them. The first deluge came in form of the noise. The chattering, semi-intelligible gossip of hundreds—no, *thousands*—of citizens who wormed and squeezed between each other on both sides of the central avenue blended into a drone more noxious than an overcrowded, swarming beehive. Only when the Trojans stopped to gawk at Philos and his companions, wrinkling their noses, did any of their babbling pause for even a second.

On stone platforms interspersed among the marketplace stalls frolicked musicians with their lyres, flutes, and drums. Philos could not make out the individual rhythms amongst the din everybody else made. He was not alone in that respect; no one else was stopping to dance to the musicians, or even dropping a single talent of gold into the bowls laid down. What was the point of making music if your audience couldn't hear you?

He leaned his head as close to Itaweret's ear as possible without touching her skin. "At least you should feel more at home here, girl of Per-Pehu."

She blinked at him. "If only that were so. I don't wish to be rude to our escorts, but compared to my home city, this place seems . . . how shall I put it? Run-down and gritty? Our place was nowhere near so, so . . . hideous!"

Since he had only heard of the Kemetian colony rather than visiting it, Philos could not adequately compare it to Troy. Nor could he disagree with Itaweret's assessment of their current surroundings. Stacked upon one another like children's clay blocks, the cubic houses of mudbrick might leave him awestruck were they not slathered brown with grime and scratchy graffiti. And those were the few structures that did not have off-white plaster peeling off everywhere. So oppressive was the miasma of odors from human sweat and filth that Philos would have preferred hanging around the sheep and cattle back in Taurocephalus.

A pair of naked children, both mottled brown with dirt and less pleasant substances, scurried across the road between Philos and the others. One of the Trojan guards barked a threatening command at them, but they had already disappeared into the shadows of an alleyway.

"You can see we also have a big crime problem on our hands," the Trojan captain said. "There's nary a street in this city that isn't polluted with beggars, pick-pockets, and loiterers. Even the nobles' districts aren't all safe."

"Odd, I didn't see those kids carrying off anything," Philos said.

"Maybe not right then, but urchins will always be urchins."

"Pardon me, sir, but *why* does your city have so much crime, as you say?" Nebta asked. "Have times been so tough lately?"

"If you ask me, I'd say it's the same reason we have so many damned foreigners camping outside. We have been too generous, too merciful to everyone. And we've been paying the price for that ever since."

Itaweret frowned. "I don't know about that. Your men weren't treating that woman and her children with tenderness, from what I saw."

The captain twirled around, baring his teeth. "Look here, Kemetian, we're doing whatever we can to correct the mistakes of our past leadership. We have been blessed that our current king is nothing like his mushy-hearted predecessor. He, more than any ruler we have had in centuries, shall make Troy great again. Speaking of the king, we're almost at his door."

The avenue ended at the mouth of a second gatehouse. This stretched even higher, by at least one third, than the gatehouse they had entered before. On each of its turrets reared an embedded stone relief of a horse kicking its forelegs, the gold-painted mane scintillating with sunlight.

"What's with you Trojans and horses, anyway?" Philos said.

Nebta hissed from the corner of her mouth, "You might want to stop giving them a hard time with your questions."

The captain nodded with a narrow, toothy grin. "Listen to your friend there, country boy. Then you might even get out of this one alive . . ."

His wicked laugh almost suppressed the creaking sound of the second gate's opening.

What drifted past the doors was not more of the stench of squalor. Instead, the fresh scents of pine mixed with flowers beckoned Itaweret into Troy's inner districts.

No longer did her feet tread on the trampled grit that had passed for pavement in the outer city. On the other side of the inner gate, dust and gravel gave way to smoother blocks of polished marble, with vibrant green lawns of thick grass and manicured bushes running alongside the paths. Palm, olive, and cypress trees cast cooling shade down from the branches and fronds as they spread overhead.

The double-story buildings among the forested gardens carried the same squarish shapes as the houses of the city beyond, but any similarities ended there. Bright shades of copper-red, yellow, and turquoise fringed every structure's upper parapets, their walls and columned faces assembled from marble of an even whiter color than the pavement on the inner streets. All bore carved images of horses on their faces, with an occasional bull or deer (or whatever the Achaeans called those antelope with horns forked like branches) inserted between the equines for variety.

Philos was right. The Trojans were more than a little preoccupied with those zebras without stripes.

They arrived at a series of roads that converged at a pool with lotus flowers, its water fed by a tiny stream trickling between the legs of another marble horse rearing up with its mouth open in a voiceless bray. As they approached this curious fountain, Philos and Bek exploded into laughter while Nebta giggled behind her hand.

Itaweret could only snort with disgust. "I expected the boys to find it funny, Nebta, but surely a woman like *you* would have better taste."

"I'm so sorry, my sister," Nebta said. "When you hang around men as much as I have over the years, you can't help but soak up their style of humor."

The Trojan captain nodded with a broad, mischievous grin. "Plus, water is what gives us life, isn't it? It's only natural that we liken it to—"

Turning away from the sight of the horse fountain, Itaweret retched, a foul air entering her mouth. "Good gods, you're making it worse. Carry on, please!"

Beyond the opposite side, the road ended at a series of steps ascending to a columned gallery. They stood in front of a double-story mansion twice as large as any of the others Itaweret noticed in the city's noble district. The guards acknowledged their captain with a bow of their heads and let him through the gallery, but did not extend the same courtesy to Itaweret or any other in her party. One shook his head at her with a concerned frown while clicking his tongue, muttering something in Trojan in what sounded, to Itaweret, like a piteous tone.

A series of frescoed corridors, populated with more equine imagery, as Itaweret had come to expect, opened into a broad, columned chamber not unlike the throne chamber from which her own father had governed Per-Pehu. Even the giant painted relief on the far wall, of two Trojan soldiers facing each other with raised weapons, recalled one in Per-Pehu showing the pharaoh trampling Achaean barbarians. The one difference? The warriors in this image were not running or massacring anyone.

On a stone chair mounted on a dais between the two soldiers' feet, a Trojan man of middle years sat in a bright-blue robe and a cylindrical crown encircled by curving horns. He stroked his long black beard and arched an eyebrow as the captain bowed to him.

"May I ask who these visitors are, Captain Hektor?" the king of Troy asked.

"They all sought an audience with you, Your Highness," Hektor answered. "And, along the way, this countryside boy among them got himself into a little extra trouble. He assaulted a number of guards on behalf of a female migrant out in the shantytown."

"I can't say I regret any of it!" Philos said. "I saw them try to rip her children away. Why, O king of Troy, would you allow such cruelty to happen under your watch?"

The Trojan king's eyelids twitched. His knuckles popped under his skin on the ends of his throne's armrest. "What did you say they were doing to that migrant and her children?"

"You mean you didn't order such a thing to happen?" Itaweret asked. "I thought you were to have decreed—"

"Sorry, my king, but it's a new policy I've put into place," Hektor interjected. "We believe it'll deter new arrivals and provide an incentive to either assimilate or leave . . ."

The red-faced king slammed his fist on his throne. "I ordered no such thing! We may have more mouths coming to Troy than we can feed, but I never asked for them to receive such abuse as you and your men are apparently delivering to them. You should be ashamed of yourself, Hektor!"

"How could you turn on your own subject like this?" Hektor said. "All I sought, my king, was a means to ease the foreigner crisis on our hands. If we must resort to intimidation and force, so be it!"

"There is a difference between sternness and cruelty, my captain. End this vile 'policy' you've enacted behind my back. If not, consider your rank, if not your very citizenship here in Troy, stripped!"

The captain's eyes shrunk with anger as he bowed again. "Very well, King Alexandros. All I, as captain of your city guard, seek is your approval, after all."

Hektor and his men filed out with the swiftness of a snake slithering from trouble.

Philos wrung his hands together. "So . . . does this mean I'm no longer in trouble?"

"Maybe, maybe not," King Alexandros of Troy answered. "You *did* assault my guards, cruel and unwarranted as their actions may have been, and I can't let that go unpunished. I must decide what I am to do with you. What I ask right now is why you and these companions of yours came here in the first place? Especially the two Kemetians. The heralds told me your colony in the Achaean lands fell to Mycenae recently. Is that true?"

"That is correct," Bek said. "My father, Mahu, was lord of the colony before the Mycenaeans, led by Scylax, sacked it and killed him. Now we believe they hold what remains of our people in chains. My sister and I seek to liberate them."

"And we can only do it with your help," Itaweret said. "Your army is among the strongest in the region next to Mycenae's. You have the only force that has any chance to persuade them to free our people."

Alexandros scratched his beard and shook his head. "You wish to know the reason we have so many immigrants from afar camping outside our city? They know they can find peace here, even if they do not have good living conditions. We avoid war as much as we can, and even more so if it's none of our business. Our army keeps the peace, nothing more. That may make us an attractive sanctuary for refugees in these parts, but it also means I can't be of much aid to your cause. I am terribly sorry for that."

"You can't, or you won't?" Nebta said. "You may prefer peace whenever possible, O king of Troy, but that doesn't mean you don't have the ability to fight when other people need you."

"My lady, I have enough citizens *and* incomers draining my coffers and granaries with their various needs and wants without wasting yet more on a war with another kingdom across the sea. One thing you commoners need to appreciate is that kingship is expensive. I can't do anything I want if I can't afford it."

"Did you say all your subjects were 'draining your coffers'?" Philos asked. "We were walking past the shantytown and through the city before we were led here to ask for your assistance. Those people didn't look like they had anything to eat. Excuse me, but after seeing with our own eyes the riches of your inner city, I believe you're not nearly as hamstrung here as you claim."

"I never said I had *that* much to go around, boy."

"And what if Mycenae turns on you next?" Itaweret continued. "They could have tracked us over here, for all you or I know. In which case, you'd have no choice but to fight them."

"Not to mention that defeating them in battle would yield plenty of profit for you and your people," Nebta added. "And even everyone sitting outside—"

"Enough!" King Alexandros shouted. "I won't say it again. We are not going to intervene in your conflict with Mycenae unless we have evidence that they're a threat. Assumptions about their 'tracking' you down aren't going to suffice. Until I see cause in reconsidering, begone!"

"Very well, King Alexandros," Itaweret said. "I see you would rather let thousands outside your palace perish, whether through starvation or slavery, than lend a helping hand. What fools we were to seek assistance from such a selfish king."

They stormed out of the throne chamber, Itaweret leading the way as they headed back for their galley along the dock. She would have a long conversation with the goddess Mut that night. An exceptionally long conversation indeed.

CHAPTER TWENTY

Sennuwy knew trouble awaited her from the damage she and her enslaved companions inflicted upon their master. That trouble would come sooner or later. She had no idea when. Orion might have professed sincerity in capitulating to save what remained of his own skin, but nobody in touch with reality could count on him not to retaliate once he had slipped away from danger. Only the most ignorant fool would not expect him to report the assault to authorities when he had the chance.

She saw the forthcoming trouble. What she did not foresee, however, was the way they would punish her. Ever since the rebellion, Sennuwy had imagined Mycenaean guards gripping her arms with the strength of cold bronze and carrying her off to a public square, where they would burn her at a stake, behead her, or flog her to death for all the city to see. Perhaps they would throw her out into the wilderness to be torn apart by the wolves, bears, or lions of the Achaean countryside.

Instead, they dragged her into a temple. Rather than the coarse hands of Mycenae's city guards clutching her limbs, she found herself in the stabbing claw-like fingernails of priestesses masked with the hook-beaked faces of gold owls.

The braziers that flared between the sanguine-painted columns filled the hallway with a sweltering heat and an infernal glow like the bowels of an active volcano. The priestesses who held Sennuwy captive chanted with a warlike rhythm while in front, women slapping handheld frame drums with a frenetic rhythm led the processional. Others marched behind, trilling piercing notes on double flutes. It sounded almost like a primitive mockery of the music she played with the other priestesses in the temple of Mut at Per-Pehu.

Had these Achaeans learned how to make music from her own Kemetian people? Or did they mean to mock her culture's musical traditions with this barbaric parody?

The hall ended in front of a terraced dais that served as the center of the temple's sanctum. On the highest platform loomed a bronze colossus of a woman armed with spear and shield, a Mycenaean boar-tusk helmet seated above her flowing straight hair and an owl with outspread wings on her shoulder. Points of silver-gray light smoldered within both the giant bronze woman and the owl's eye sockets.

Before the statue's feet rested a rectangular altar with stains of blood still glistening on its stony surface. The priestesses lay Sennuwy onto the altar on her back, tightening their grip on her wrists and ankles whenever she attempted to budge her limbs. One pressed her hand over Sennuwy's mouth to muffle her screams. She promptly bit onto the flesh of the priestess's palm. "You lot are demons in human guise! You can't slaughter me like cattle here!"

A middle-aged woman shawled with a wolf's hide emerged from behind the idol. "On most nights, it *is* livestock we sacrifice here," she replied, her voice cold as the breath of death itself. "This night, however, Athena's palate demands a different flavor of flesh for a change. How about . . . *human* prey, my goddess?"

The woman in the shawl fished out a silver dagger and held it to the light of the statue's eyes. Sennuwy screamed until the blade plunged down into her heart. Her pain ended in the same flashing moment as the rest of her existence.

Kleno stepped back from the altar and bowed to Athena. "She is all yours, O gray-eyed one."

The glow in the goddess's eyes oscillated with an intensity that soon transferred to the eyes of the newly regrown owl on her shoulder. Waving tendrils of light extended down to where the Kemetian rebel's corpse bled on the altar. The rays seeped into the wound in the girl's breast, closing it until all trace of injury vanished. Even the blood gushing from it dissipated into nothing.

The Kemetian girl's eyelids parted to broadcast the same silvery light that had infiltrated her. Her body floated up from the altar without anyone touching it, spinning on its feet in mid-levitation to peer down at Kleno. Her arms spread away from the torso like a bird's outstretched wings, and her entire body, dead on the altar just a moment before, expanded until it burst through the girl's tunic.

The body's expansion continued in front of the amazed priestesses until it reached the size of a rhinoceros from the southern lands—and even larger. It then began the next stage of its transformation. Kleno laughed with eager anticipation. This time, the priestess Itaweret would need much more than a throw of a knife to stop her.

The new creature, minutes ago a rebellious and feisty Kemetian prisoner, let out a screeching roar that almost rattled the temple columns with its explosive volume.

A copse of olive trees and bushes girdled a pond at the foot of the slope south of Troy. After the sun disappeared behind the surface of the Great Green to the west, there remained only fireflies dancing over the tall grass and the glimmer of moonlit leaves to illuminate the grove. All Itaweret could hear as she approached the reed-fringed pool were the songs of crickets and frogs. It was a serenity she had come to miss since they had gotten off the boat to Troy.

She held the scepter of Mut with both hands as she examined the pond and the surrounding grove. The experience she had gained from the journey taught her never to take a moment of peace at face value. Any number of predators could be lurking in the bushy scrub outside the city, like the bear that attacked her and Bek before Xiphos intervened. Not that she could detect any sign of them, not even tracks in the dirt, but then again, she never learned or possessed the skills of an experienced woodsman.

When no wildlife emerged after several minutes of waiting, Itaweret wrung both hands on the scepter and let her thoughts drift back to the Temple of Mut in Per-Pehu.

"O goddess Mut, I have spoken to King Alexandros of Troy. I am sorry to report that he has refused to help us. What are we to do now?"

Warmth returned to the scepter, seeping through the skin of her palm as it had when she had last spoken to the goddess. Mut revealed herself, now levitating over the pond, her onyx-black arms outspread like wings. The golden aura enveloping her drove back all darkness within the grove's breadth.

"It was as I warned you, Itaweret. Pleas alone would not sway King Alexandros of Troy to your cause. Only one thing would threaten him enough to get involved, and I am sorry to say that it is something you have brought unto him."

"What do you mean, my goddess?" Itaweret asked. "We couldn't possibly have done anything to harm him."

"Oh, not intentionally, of course. Yet it remains true that Scylax and his sister Kleno know you are here and are preparing their attack. Even worse, Kleno has a new incarnation of Athena at her service, one more terrible than before. You remember your fellow priestess Sennuwy?"

"What? Don't tell me she—"

"Kleno sacrificed her to create a new incarnation, which has now taken form. Sennuwy is no more. Her flesh, bones, and soul have become those of a monster in Athena's image."

Itaweret's heart sank with the crushing weight and shock of Mut's description. If there was anyone in all Per-Pehu she could confide in outside her immediate family, it was Sennuwy. They had been friends ever since Sennuwy's mother brought her to the palace grounds for games of hide-and-seek. And what about all the hours they'd spent together braiding each other's hair beneath the tamarisk trees in the temple gardens?

Itaweret collapsed onto her knees. "That cannot be! How could that Mycenaean bitch do that to my friend? Tell me, O goddess, what am I to do?"

"The Trojans will be more than able to fend off the Mycenaean forces by themselves, but the creature Kleno has created will be another matter. Not even Xiphos the lion, try as he might, can vanquish it by himself. What you need, Itaweret, is another monster of your own to overcome Kleno's."

"Who must I sacrifice to summon that one? My brother? Philos? Nebta? Even myself?"

The goddess descended onto the bank of the pond and placed both of her hands on Itaweret's shoulders. Her divine touch gave off the balmy heat of a bright summer day. "There are many more ways to bring such creatures to life than blood sacrifice, my child. Allow me to point you down another path." She paused for a moment. "Anpu, I summon ye!"

She pointed her arms to a flashing burst of gold light. It swirled and formed itself into the body of Anpu, the black jackal-masked god of the dead. He knelt before Itaweret, a tiny human skeleton resting with crossed arms on his hands.

When Anpu spoke, a dog-like growl underlaid his voice. "You know what happens to those who depart from this world, daughter of Mahu. But do you know what happens to their bodies when they are buried?"

"Yes, they must be embalmed," Itaweret said. "Otherwise, their *ka* and the *ba* cannot reunite at night within the tomb."

"But what if they are buried without the embalming?"

"I do not know."

"In many other cultures, Itaweret, the dead are buried in the earth without a coffin or even linen wrappings. In some cases, they may rot into oblivion, or a jackal or other scavenger might dig up their corpse and devour them. Yet, if neither of those things happen, and the bones remain in the earth long enough, they may turn to stone like the soil around them."

The skeleton in Anpu's hands transformed into dark-gray stone. "In layers of rock across the world, there lie myriad bones and skeletons belonging to creatures of the distant past, all of them having become stone long ago," he continued. "Many of these beasts were far mightier and more terrible than anything you mortals can imagine today."

Itaweret turned to Mut, and then to Anpu. "Is that what you want me to bring to life?" she asked. "Some monster that died hundreds of years ago?"

"Think more than a few hundred years, mortal. Think of thousands, or millions, or even a few hundred million years. Did you, in fact, know that the world is far, far older than even that?"

"Do not overwhelm her with your revelations, Anpu," Mut interjected. "Itaweret, lead your friends into the hills east of here. Look for a cave with bones of stone embedded in its walls. One of these shall provide you with a monster more than capable of defeating Kleno's."

"How do I know which cave to search?" Itaweret asked. "For all we know, there could be hundreds of caves in those hills!"

"There are also many villages. Some of the people will know of a cave. You only need to ask around . . . someone there will know."

"One more thing before we go," Anpu said. He pressed his palms together, and then parted them to produce a bronze pickax and trowel in place of the petrified skeleton. "These will help you dig out the bones. Be careful, though, as the bones can be quite brittle."

He laid both tools on the grass at Itaweret's feet. The gods disappeared upon a flicker of light.

Itaweret picked up the pickax, lighter than she had expected. "Looks like we have a lot of work to do, and only a little time to do it," she said to herself.

CHAPTER TWENTY-ONE

By the time Itaweret returned to the docks, the Phoenician sailors had finished setting up their encampment on the beach. Dozens of cooking fires in front of the clustered tents merged to form a giant orange beacon that wavered throughout the night to the rhythm of their drunken shanties, some of the glow reflecting in slivers of surf that slid back and forth over the sand.

Itaweret found her brother and friends gathered on stools around a fire near the edge of camp. Philos fed a leg of roast pig to Xiphos, who devoured it with the rapid enthusiasm of a lion that spent way too many days eating fish on the open sea. Bek and Nebta sat closer together than Itaweret had seen them before, Bek's arm wrapped around the Wawatian woman's shoulder.

"I see you two have grown even closer while I was away," Itaweret said.

Nebta rose to meet the approaching Itaweret. "Oh, we simply needed to keep each other cozy during the evening. Now, where have you been? I was getting worried for you."

"I told you, I needed a moment to speak to my goddess. It didn't take as long as I expected. For one, we now have a new destination in our quest."

"What would it be this time?" Bek asked. "We all saw that going to Troy didn't turn out as well as we hoped."

Philos looked toward the pickax and trowel, both of which Itaweret carried under her arms. "Would it have something to do with those digging tools? Where did you get those?"

"The gods gave them to us," Itaweret said. "They told me that, somewhere in the hills to the east, there is a cave with the bones of ancient beasts embedded in its rock. If we dig some of them out, we could bring one of those beasts back to life to fight Scylax's forces by our side."

"Why would we need a monster for that?" Nebta asked.

Itaweret paused. "Because Scylax has a monster of his own again. His sister created it from the blood of one of my friends in the priesthood. That is what Mut told me."

Everyone gasped in horror. "That can't be!" Bek exclaimed. "Is he also planning to attack us here at Troy?"

"I am afraid so," Itaweret said. "That's why we need to head into the hills and find those bones as soon as we can."

"Do you even know exactly where this cave is?" Nebta asked. "There's got to be dozens or even hundreds of them up in the hills. Surely your gods would be able to point out which one we should search."

"I know, but all they told me is to ask the villagers we meet. They might know if there's a special cave with big bones inside."

Nebta grunted. "Then you better hope the locals there are friendlier than the Trojans. Regardless, I'm sorry to say I can't go with you. I have to keep an eye out on my men while they rest and restock."

"And I will help her with that," Bek said.

Itaweret beat the ground with the scepter. "What? I can't do this on my own. There might be wild animals out there, or bandits, or the gods know what else! You wouldn't want to leave your sister defenseless, would you?"

Nebta chuckled. "Oh, c'mon, if you can slay a giant owl, you're tougher than you think you are."

Philos rose from his stool, staff in hand, while stroking his lion's mane behind the ears. "Xiphos and I will go with you, Itaweret. Not only might it be dangerous out there, but I wouldn't want you to have to do all that digging by yourself."

Itaweret smirked. "I certainly wouldn't mind help with that part. Now, since we don't have a lot of time before the Mycenaeans show up on these shores, you and I should leave here as soon as we can. Let us say, early next morning?"

"One more question," Nebta said. "What happens if your journey takes so long that the Mycenaeans get here before you find your beast?"

"It shouldn't. Please, all I can ask is that you have faith in us, like you have faith in the gods."

"Sorry, but I'll need more than mere faith to trust that you can do this before it's too late."

"We don't have many choices left," Philos said. "I don't know about you, but I'd sooner gamble on this working out than sit here like a hopeless coward and watch Scylax burn the world down."

Nebta shook her head with a sigh. "Fine. You win. But you and Itaweret better come back with a monster that will impress me."

No more words passed between them. Philos went into the nearest tent and pulled out a fourth stool, for Itaweret. She acknowledged his gesture with a smile and sat. When she first met the young shepherd, Itaweret had assumed him to be an uncouth, uncultured barbarian like all the other Achaeans. To see him show such courtesy, honor, and courage meant that he could be so much more. Maybe she was wrong about the barbarians. They might look different and speak a different language, but they were still human beings, every bit as intelligent and caring as her own people. They too could be as noble as any Kemetians.

Regardless of his rustic upbringing, she thought, Philos would make a fine king of Mycenae. But who would his queen be? Who would give birth to his heir?

Itaweret nudged her stool toward Philos and let him place his arm around her. When their skin made contact, her chest warmed like the campfire before them. She leaned her head into his shoulder.

CHAPTER TWENTY-TWO

The red claws of dawn scratched the sky with the blare of a trumpet and the rumble of war drums. Scylax of Mycenae marched from his palace entrance in full panoply to the plaza adjoining it, where his finest soldiers gathered into a thick mass of shimmering bronze and flowing red helmet-crests. Alongside the king walked his sister, with the breath of the creature falling like steam on the nape of Scylax's neck. Most men would have found that a terrifying sensation, yet the heat comforted him in a strange way against the chill of the dying night.

Scylax tilted his head back, thrust his chest up under his armor, and cleared his throat before his audience.

"Morning, brave warriors of Mycenae. I have gathered you here to alert you of a newfound threat against our proud city. We have at last learned the whereabouts of the priestess Itaweret, daughter of the fallen great chief of Per-Pehu. She and her allies have fled across the wine-dark sea to Troy, where she doubtless is plotting her revenge for our conquering her people's intrusive colony.

"Men of Mycenae, we cannot allow this elusive Kemetian wench to remain free and safe, lest her scheming bring our civilization to its downfall. We must do everything we can to subdue her and anyone who supports her, even if we must resort to putting her to the sword. That is why I, your king, have chosen to bring you to the very walls of Troy itself. If the Trojans do not turn the priestess over to our control, we will have no choice but to destroy them as we have destroyed Per-Pehu!"

One of the soldiers raised his hand up. "Pardon me, sire, but how do we know the Trojans mean to protect this woman? Perhaps they will have no qualm giving her up?"

"Why, that's the very reason we'll demand they turn her over before we attack!" Scylax answered. "Do you mean to question my wisdom, soldier?"

"Don't misunderstand me, my king, I shall serve you to the end. It's only that it hasn't been long at all since we came home from Per-Pehu. You mean to bring us back to the warpath already?"

Scylax pulled his sword out of its scabbard, a shriek of scraping metal, then slashed it into the air. "Don't you dare be a coward before me. The future of Mycenae is at stake. Let the Kemetian witch have her way, and our entire civilization will be ground to dust. Are you not with me?"

The soldiers straightened in silence.

"Good. Then to Troy we shall go. And if they will not listen to reason from us, then they shall listen to the butchery of their men and the wailing of their women!"

The king of Mycenae waved his sword again, and the soldiers crowed out their war cry. Behind him, Kleno's monster drew back its beaked head with a great screeching roar.

The cry of a hawk bounced between bright marble-white cliffs studded with boulders and shrubby vegetation. Itaweret sat on one of the outcroppings underneath a cedar tree to wipe the perspiration off her forehead, giving her sore legs a shake. The group spent the whole morning hiking up the valley underneath the burning glare of the sun, burdened by the pickax and trowel slung to their backs. It was like trudging through the hills around Taurocephalus all over again, except in this region, there were not so many trees to provide shade.

Philos, also slathered with sweat, seated himself next to her on the rock, with Xiphos curling his body around them. Itaweret handed Philos the water-skin they had brought from the camp and let him wash his face with its contents.

Philos grumbled. "I would ask how far the nearest village is, except neither of us would know that. Gods, we don't even know if they would understand our language."

"They might understand us if they're related to the Trojans," Itaweret said. "I wouldn't give up hope yet. It's all we have."

Xiphos cocked his head up with a low growl and a twitch of his tail. "What is it, Xiphos?" Philos asked.

Itaweret looked down the slope in the same direction the lion faced. A chill flowed down her cheeks as the blood drained from them. "I think we have company."

A gang of men in buckskin loincloths clambered up the hill. They were all brown-skinned with black hair streaming in curly waves from their heads. Their eyes gleamed bright blue with hostile intent. They yelled in an unrecognizable language while brandishing hatchets and spears crafted from wood, bone, and flint.

Dark skin and blue eyes . . . a combination she had heard about and seen once before, only once . . . but when and where?

Xiphos bared his fangs while holding his ground. He roared at the approaching tribesmen. They halted and stepped back, murmuring among themselves while holding their primitive weapons close.

"They look like those Pelasgians," Philos said. "Never would I have imagined there'd still be some left alive. They're supposed to be extinct!"

The foremost of the men was a tall, brawny man with silver ornaments hanging alongside the fangs and claws of his necklace. He pointed an ax fashioned from a boar's jawbone at Itaweret and Philos. "Who are you two to trespass on our lands?" he growled in Trojan.

"Your lands? How would we know these are your lands?" Philos asked.

With a confused grunt, the Pelasgian leader withdrew his jawbone ax. "You're not from anywhere near here, are you?"

"No, we both come from quite far away," Itaweret said. "We mean none of your people any harm. Please trust us."

"That is what they all say, before they break in and steal from us!" another Pelasgian said. "How do we know you are any different?"

"What exactly are people stealing from you?" Philos asked. "I know your people have been through a lot of trouble in the last few thousand years, what with us Achaeans and so many others taking your land, but why would anyone dare molest you now?"

The leader held up one of his necklace's silver pieces between his fingers. "They are greedier for our shining white stone than wolves are for carrion. Once the Trojans even forced us to dig it up for them, but we fought our way back to freedom. And we shall kill anyone who seeks to pry more of it from our land!"

"We can assure you that we have no interest in your silver whatsoever," Itaweret said. "What we're looking for are bones. Really old bones since turned to stone, hidden in a cave somewhere in this area."

The Pelasgians looked at one another, scratching their heads and muttering among themselves. Would people from such a primitive culture even know what she meant? Itaweret wondered. Maybe they discovered some of those bones while digging for silver all that time ago.

"We know what you are talking about," the lead warrior said. "But the cave you describe is *sacred* to us. We'd sooner have you steal the shining stones than anything in there."

"Sacred, you say?" Philos said. "Then why don't you ask your gods for permission to take the bones from them? It can't be that big a deal for them."

"You know nothing about our 'gods,' outlander! And what of these bones of stone? How much do you need them?"

"Why, nothing less than the fate of the world depends on it!" Itaweret said. "From across the sea, there's a cruel chieftain named Scylax who plans to invade this area with an army of thousands. He has the most terrible monster under his control, or so my gods tell me. We need those bones to assemble a monster of our own. Otherwise, Scylax and his minions will overrun this place. Imagine what he'll do to your people."

"Why should we believe all of this?" another of the Pelasgian warriors asked. "How do we know you're not trying to trick us?"

Philos groaned. "Why would we? For the love of all the gods, have some faith in us!"

A suggestion ran through Itaweret's mind, onto her lips. "How about we offer you something in return? Your people have been stuck in these winding valleys for who knows how many generations. Don't you want a better home than that?"

"Where else could we live?" the Pelasgian leader said. "The Trojans have claimed almost the whole coast west of here. And we'd rather not settle in land claimed by others."

"I know of a place beyond the other side of the sea where your people could live. It was the city I grew up in, but Scylax has turned it into a smoking ruin and carried off its people as slaves. Maybe you could settle on the coast where my city once stood?"

"Itaweret, what on earth are you proposing?" Philos asked. "You mean to offer your own home to them? Then where would your people live once you free them?"

"My brother and I will figure that out later. For now, since nobody lives in Per-Pehu anymore, it should be safe for these Pelasgians to take."

The leader of the Pelasgian troop stroked his chin and nodded. "That is the most generous offer any outlanders have ever given us. You promise to uphold this offer once you have received what you want?"

Itaweret bowed her head to him. "I promise."

"Then I, Triopas of the Deer Clan, shall invite you to our village. Follow us and stay close. Wolves and leopards abound in these hills."

Philos rubbed Xiphos's mane, then his head. "At least we have protection of our own against those."

Itaweret looked up to the tip of Mut's scepter, which shone more brightly in the sunlight. She hoped that, in offering and pledging the city that had once been hers to these strange people, she was not making a terrible mistake.

CHAPTER TWENTY-THREE

The valley widened into a grassy plain, its blades high enough to tickle Itaweret's knees. A herd of roe deer galloped into a copse of trees as she and her companions followed the Pelasgian tribesmen down a game trail. The roe deer looked rather like gazelles, with white spots and horns that branched like tree limbs.

"How do you never run out of deer to hunt?" Itaweret asked. "You must've lived in this area for so many generations."

"We don't get all our food from hunting like our forefathers did," Triopas said. "We grow some of it instead, like the Trojans do."

He gestured to an area where the thick wild grass gave way to yellow shoots of wheat and barley. The tilled and farmed plots were adjoined by rows of olive and palm trees. They sat alongside a brook that gurgled across the plain. Over the stream's edge, a flock of bleating sheep gathered, bleating a little louder as they drank.

Philos's eyes shone as he inhaled through his nose. "It's almost like my own home."

Itaweret took in the scent of sheep dung and damp earth, grimacing. "No offense, but it certainly smells like it."

A crude bridge of wooden planks connected the brook's two banks. Beyond the opposite shore, there lay a cluster of dome-shaped hovels with hides piled over walls built of sticks and large animal bones. In front of the ramshackle homes, more Pelasgians sat around cooking fires. At the front of the village stood a pole topped with a deer's skull, with sheets of buckskin hanging from its antlers.

"Welcome to the village of the Deer Clan," Triopas said.

As Itaweret and Philos followed him past the village's standard, the locals looked up from their fires to eye them with the same suspicious curiosity that the people of Taurocephalus had shown. The women also held onto their children, while the men held onto them in turn. This time, however, nobody uttered a word to the newcomers that could be interpreted as insulting or hostile. The Pelasgians may have felt little reason to trust strangers, but they felt little reason to fear them as well.

At the edge of the village stood a hut twice as wide as the others, shaded by leafy tendrils of the willow tree overhanging it. Another deer's skull sat above this hut's entrance, with a pair of human skulls perched beside it. The hairs on the back of Itaweret's neck prickled when she noticed the macabre detail.

"This would be the home of our shaman, Zugutan," Triopas said. "You need not worry; she's nowhere near as sinister as you seem to expect."

"Oh, we're not afraid or anything," Philos said. "It's only that we've been raised to regard priests of any kind with the utmost respect. Right, Itaweret?"

Itaweret nodded. "Then maybe I should be the one to speak to her."

As she walked toward the hut, a plethora of strange odors struck her nose and made her wince. She could hear the muffled drone of a woman's voice coming from within the domicile. After wringing her hands around Mut's scepter, Itaweret pushed the buckskin hide flap over the entrance and poked her head inside.

Within the hut, surrounded by pots and baskets holding substances from which the odd smells had originated, a woman not much older than Itaweret sat cross-legged on the floor. Cloaked in a bearskin, black marks tattooed all over her face and a necklace of bear claws and silver disks hanging to her chest, the shaman rolled her head around with shut eyes. Silver and bone ringlets that adorned her locks of hair jangled.

"May I please speak to you, if you are the shaman?" Itaweret asked.

Zugutan's eyes flashed open, glaring at her with a furious scowl as she jumped back. "Who are you to interrupt my trance?"

"I apologize, O Zugutan. Triopas sent me to you. I come from far away and do not know everything about your customs. All I seek is a little help."

"You're one of those outlanders, aren't you? What help could you possibly want from our people?"

"My home village has been destroyed. The man who destroyed it is hunting me down. He has a monster helping his cause, and the only way I can defeat him is by raising a monster of my own. To do that, I will need some old bones of stone from a cave in this area."

"You mean from the cave of our ancestors. I am sorry; I cannot allow that. It is sacred ground. An outlander like you breaking into it would provoke our ancestors' anger and bring who knows what kind of disastrous woe upon us."

"How do you know they would do that?"

With frightening speed, Zugutan shot her hand out and slapped Itaweret on the cheek. "Don't you dare question our traditions, outlander! The point is, you must stay away from our sacred places."

"What if we promised you something in return? We know of good land, far beyond the other side of the great sea, which will provide far more for your people than this valley ever could. And you would be safe from Trojans and others who might molest you."

"False bribes like that won't work with me. Nor will they work with our ancestors. Begone, already!"

Itaweret found herself stumped. She needed *something* to persuade this shaman to let her and Philos visit that cave. If the promise of new land would not work, what could?

Wait, if outlanders were absolutely forbidden from entering the cave, then . . .

"Could it perhaps be *your* people who dig those bones out for us?" Itaweret asked. "Might your ancestors not mind if it is your people, and not outlanders, doing the work?"

Zugutan shook her head, her laugh loud and mocking. "You mean like how the Trojans wanted us to dig up silver for them? You think us so foolish as to fall for *that* again?"

"We're not trying to exploit your people, O Zugutan. We mean to save my people, and maybe the world as we know it. Please understand, ever since he destroyed our home, the Mycenaean king Scylax has forced what remains of my people into slavery. He will probably do the same to anyone who stands in the way of his ambitions. Including your own people."

Zugutan's features softened, the distrust in her eyes doused. She sighed. "If that is true, then I should talk with the ancestors about it. They might make an exception for you, this once. But I cannot promise it."

"Very well," Itaweret said. "Let us know when they have spoken. Thank you very much."

She left the hut to rejoin the others outside. "What did she say?" Philos asked. "It sounded like there was quite an argument in there."

Itaweret nodded. "There was, believe me. She told me she would consult the spirits of her ancestors about it. Until then, we must wait."

Zugutan pinched a dab of ground cannabis from one of her medicine bowls and inserted it into her boar-tusk pipe. Lighting the pipe with her cooking fire, she leaned back and inhaled the odoriferous fumes, letting them lift her consciousness off the earth and into the realm of the ancestors.

Soon, the ancestors appeared to her as silvery faces in the smoke, filling the entire interior of the hut as they looked down upon her with radiant eyes. Scattered among them were the likenesses of her mother and father, her grandparents, aunts and uncles as she remembered them from childhood, and those from generations of the Deer Clan who had lived and departed long before she was born. Tears came to her eyes as she looked around and saw all of them gathered.

"Ancestors, hear me out," she began. "There is an outlander woman who has approached me with a plea on behalf of her people. She claims that, in order to free them, she must bring to life a monster using bones taken from the Cave of Bones."

The ancestors silently considered Zugutan's request, knowing she never summoned them from the other side unless a matter was of grave importance to their people. They looked at each other, wisdom flowing between them like rays of light, then nodded.

When they spoke, their voices combined in a resonant, booming unison. "Yes, we have seen and heard her. We can say that she speaks the truth. You have no cause to distrust her."

"I do not understand. Do you not want the outlanders to stay away from your sacred spaces?"

"This one means no harm. All she desires is freedom for her own people, and to eliminate a grave threat to the world. That is why you must bring her to the cave. Disregard our advice at the peril of all our people."

Zugutan knelt on the floor. "O ancestors, I meant no disrespect. All I ask is, why would our own people suffer if this outlander does not have what she wants?"

"Understand that her enemy, Scylax of Mycenae, wants to bring all the known world under his thumb of bronze. You cannot expect any mercy from him. If you do not help stop him, he will destroy us all."

The light emanating from the ancestors' faces turned yellowish orange like a raging fire. The hut warmed until it resembled a sweltering oven. Men hollered and women shrieked beneath the roar of the flames, perishing in the body of the vision.

"No, I cannot let that happen!" Zugutan said. "I hear you, ancestors. I will lead the outlander woman to the cave. You have my word."

The faces of the ancestors dissipated as the smoke cleared, and the temperature within the hut cooled back to normal. Never would Zugutan have imagined that the ancestors would be so willing to let outlanders into their sacred domain. It challenged everything she understood from her years of communing with them. Perhaps it was as her mother had said when she passed down the shaman's mantle to her daughter: No matter how much you thought you knew the ancestors, they always had something new to teach you.

Zugutan poked her head through her hut's entrance, whistling to the outlander woman and the lighter-skinned man who waited next to her. "The ancestors have spoken. Follow me."

CHAPTER TWENTY-FOUR

Three megalithic arches stood in a semicircle outside the cave, which gaped into the hills at the valley's southern end. Embedded within the arches' giant sandstone blocks were hunks of darker brown rock shaped like fragments of bone. As she glided her hands on their surfaces, Itaweret could not identify what sort of creatures perished and hardened into these bone-like hunks. Some of the petrified bones reached, or even surpassed, the size of hippopotamus or elephant bones.

What sort of giant beasts roamed the earth so many thousands or millions of years ago?

"Why don't we knock over those big rocks and mine the bones out of them right here?" Philos asked. "We wouldn't even have to go into the cave then."

Zugutan shot him an angry look. "Don't you even think about it!"

"Alright. Sorry."

"You are talking about the realm of our ancestors. Show them some respect!"

"By the mercy of the gods, let that be an end to the bickering," Itaweret said. She turned to Philos. "We need Zugutan to guide us, so whatever you do, please listen to her."

They entered the cave together, following Zugutan, who carried a torch. Like the cave near Taurocephalus, painted illustrations of people and wildlife covered the walls. This time, Itaweret was not that interested. She paid more attention to the spaces in the rock between the paintings.

"So far, I don't see any bones in here," Philos said. "Only more of these old drawings."

"You have to go deeper into the cave for the bones," Zugutan said. "Much deeper."

Xiphos lowered himself to the cave floor and growled. Zugutan retreated from him and stood behind Philo, a slight tremble shimmering through her body. "That big lion of yours doesn't mean to attack, does he?" she asked.

"Oh, he won't hurt you," Philos said. "I think one of the paintings has him spooked. What's the matter, boy?"

Xiphos faced a painting of a giant four-legged creature. It was like an elephant in most respects, except its tusks curved downward from the tip of its lower jaw. The animal's trunk rose overhead in a threatening manner, as if trumpeting in a murderous rampage.

"Don't worry, Xiphos, it's only a drawing," Philos said. "Though of what, I have no idea."

"Whatever it is, its remains might be inside here," Itaweret said.

Many of the other paintings also took the forms of creatures unlike anything Itaweret had seen, in art or in the flesh. A flock of giant ostrich-like birds, their beaks hooked like falcons, ran across the cave wall in pursuit of herds of deer or antelope, their apparent intent predatory. She noticed rhinoceroses with forked horns, slender and serpentine whales with two pairs of flippers, and tiny, zebra-like animals with paws like dogs, instead of hooves. All over the walls stood big, roaring cats with oversized upper canines that better resembled daggers or sabers than teeth.

Deeper inside, the paintings and drawings gave way to scattered lumps of darker rock sticking out of the walls. Xiphos trotted up to one of the chunks, shaped like a long, thin leg bone. He licked it while pawing at its edges.

Philos chuckled. "Poor thing thinks it's a bone he can chew on!"

"It is indeed a bone," Zugutan said. "Though even he would break his teeth if he tried to bite it."

Most of the dark fragments were too small and jumbled to recall anything that Itaweret could recognize. Yet mixed among them were objects that were easily identifiable. *Bones.* Some were the tiny skeletons of fish or other aquatic creatures, but the rest appeared to be ribs, limbs, and skulls of larger animals.

Itaweret ran her fingers over the forked horn of a creature like one of the strange rhinos she had seen in the paintings. She and her allies might raise an entire army of monsters from this treasure trove of bones, more than enough to trample Scylax's entire army. The problem? Controlling all the beasts after they were brought back to life. And what would she do with all the reborn beasts once the war was over?

She thought about it and shook her head. She could handle one monster at a time. That was all.

"Whoa, look at how humongous this one is!" Philos said. "Why don't we dig it out?"

He ran his finger along the elongated skull of a creature embedded in the cave wall. It stretched longer than the height of a man from snout to back. Two curved, sword-sized tusks curved backward from the tip of its lower jaw.

"I don't think the three of us could carry that thing back out by ourselves," Itaweret said.

Philos unslung the pickax from his back. "No problem. We'll only take half of it instead. They didn't say we needed the whole animal's body, did they?"

"Considering most of these other bones have been broken up into pieces, that would be next to impossible anyway."

Philos struck the cave wall next to the giant skull with the pickax. The moment the tool's head contacted the rock, a deep crack ran from the point of impact all around the skull, forming an outline of glowing golden light around the petrified bone. He stammered something unintelligible, falling back in shock.

"What in the spirits' name did that 'pickax' tool just do?" Zugutan asked.

"It's a gift from our gods," Itaweret replied. "That must be its special power."

"I'd say."

Zugutan wedged the trowel into the crack underneath the creature's skull. It took only a single pull backward for the entire skull to roll out and tumble onto the floor, breaking into two.

Philos laughed. "At least we don't have to worry about digging through that rock for hours!"

Together, the three hauled the big skull's front half out of the cave and deposited it under the shadow of the three megalithic arches. The stone of bone was so heavy that, even with all the help, Itaweret worried her own arm bones would snap under its weight.

Now to transform this partial hunk of a monstrous creature's head into a whole, living animal. How to do that?

Itaweret held onto the scepter of Mut with both hands. "O goddess, we have obtained the bone of our monster. Please show us how we can bring it to life."

The goddess's light beamed out of the scepter's top. The ray of light bent down to the half-skull and expanded to bathe its whole mass. Radiating golden sunlight all around it, the half-skull rose from the ground until it hung in the air, higher than an elephant's head. Spots of white bone appeared and expanded over its surface until it replaced all of the brown stone.

From its back end grew the entire remainder of the skull. The creature's spinal vertebrae and ribs began to extend outward, which in turn sprouted four columnar legs to support the materializing skeleton. Vital organs filled in the cavity between the ribs, while tentacles of muscular flesh wrapped around and covered the bones. A wrinkled yellow-gray hide spread across the newly created skeleton, encasing it.

They looked at the newly formed creature, their mouths open. In front of them stood an elephant over a third taller and more gigantic than any Itaweret had seen before. It differed from other elephants in ways besides its sheer size. Its long and sharp tusks ran backward from the tip of its lower jaw, as they had in the skull Philos dug out of the cave wall.

Flapping its broad ears like fans, the creature came alive, swaying its head sideways and surveying its surroundings until its gaze met the alarmed eyes of Xiphos.

The elephant raised a foreleg and rumbled, spreading its ears outward. Xiphos lowered himself to the ground and roared back at the beast. "Stay down, Xiphos," Philos said calmly. He turned to Itaweret. "You know any way to control that thing?"

"Let me try," Zugutan said.

She strode up to the elephant and placed her hand on its trunk, murmuring words in a language Itaweret could not understand. The creature folded its ears back as its threatening rumble ceased.

"She is confused," Zugutan said. "She doesn't know where she is or what we are. The lion frightens her."

"You can read her mind?" Itaweret asked.

"I can speak to her. It's what we shamans do. Why don't you try to talk to her?"

Itaweret touched the elephant on the trunk, gripping the scepter of Mut tightly in her other hand. She closed her eyes and whispered reassuring words in Kemetian. The staff burned warm in her grip.

Before her eyes, a vision of a verdant semitropical forest flashed over the landscape. She beheld other elephants with tusks on their jaws, ambling about between the buttress roots of immense jungle trees, while chattering chimpanzee-like apes watched from the treetop canopy overhead. The steamy humidity of the forest drove out the drier air that Itaweret knew from the valley before.

"You're looking into her memories," Zugutan said. "This is the world she knew before she died."

Itaweret stroked the elephant's skin and looked up into her glossy wet eyes. She and the elephant silently shared their understanding of what it was like to lose your home forever.

The sight, sounds, and mist of the jungle faded away, returning to the area between the cave and the megaliths.

"Do not worry, big girl," Itaweret said to the elephant. "The world you knew is gone, but you shall live again. All we need in repayment is your help."

"So now that you have a pet elephant from a bygone age, what are you going to call her?" Philos asked.

"Hmmm . . . I shall name her after my late mother, Dedyet. Wouldn't that be an honorable name, Dedyet?"

The massive elephant raised her trunk to the sky and trumpeted.

CHAPTER TWENTY-FIVE

A salt-scented breeze pulled onto the frizzy mass of black hair that grew atop Bek's scalp during the journey. As he strolled along the beach, he picked up stones and tossed them into an ocean that had turned dark gray beneath an overcast sky. The howl of the wind and hiss of the surf suppressed the vulgar banter coming from the distant sailors' camp, loud noises of ocean and nature that he appreciated. It was not that he never liked joking or singing with Nebta's Phoenician crew. Uncouth and crass as they could be, the sailors were not always the most unpleasant company. Yet neither could he bring himself to sit in one spot the whole time until his sister returned with their new monster. If he could only idle away in the meantime, he might as well get his feet moving for the shortest moment.

A thin split in the clouds sent in a sheet of morning sunlight, which fell upon the beach behind him. The rays landed on Nebta, giving her dark skin a radiant sheen as she smiled at him.

"Sorry if I'm intruding into your solitude," Nebta said.

Bek smirked back at her. "I don't mind at all if it's you."

She stood beside him and threw a handful of sand at the water much as he had been throwing the stones. Her other hand drifted toward his until they locked together in a mutual grip.

"Have you given any thought as to how we're going to beat this Scylax once he arrives?" she asked. "Your sister's monster couldn't possibly be enough to beat his whole army, could it? Especially since the Mycenaeans supposedly have a monster of their own."

"I suppose it depends on how big our monster's going to be compared to theirs."

"I say we give the king of Troy another try. We could never defeat the Mycenaean army without his aid, monster or no monster."

"You heard what he had to say last time. He showed no desire to get involved in the conflict whatsoever. There's no way we can change his mind."

Nebta shrugged. "Why don't we, say, offer him something in return? I don't know what that would be, but *something* . . ."

"What could we, of all people, have to offer a king of high-walled Troy? We have neither land nor any other form of wealth of our own. We have nothing. Let's face it, the Mycenaeans will destroy us all while the Trojans sit back and watch."

"That's the thing, Bek. Maybe they won't sit back. Scylax wants to conquer the whole world, does he not? I don't think the king of Troy would want to submit to him, either."

"He might, though, if Scylax promises not to lay a finger on his people while going after us."

Bek sighed as he threw another rock. The sunlit fissure in the clouds had closed, turning the world gray again. Even the gods in the heavens sensed how hopeless the situation had become, he thought.

"Let us assume we did figure out a way to beat the Mycenaeans," Nebta said. "What will we do then?"

"Oh, that's part's easy," Bek said. "I will lead the people of Per-Pehu back to our city's ruins and have it rebuilt. Then I will take my father's place as great chief of the colony. And I know exactly who I want to reign beside me as my queen."

He nodded at her and smiled.

She chuckled while bumping her hand against Bek's. "You mean how Philos would like your sister to reign beside him?"

"Exactly."

The next sound Bek heard stunned him. It was a massive trumpeting call, an elephant, louder than any he'd heard before, sounding off from the hills behind the beach.

Itaweret and Zugutan rode Dedyet to a stand of date palm trees along the beach's inland edge. Behind them were Philos and Xiphos, followed by the warrior Triopas and a troop of armed comrades. They reached the shoreline to find Bek and Nebta gawking at them, jaws dropped open and locked in place.

Itaweret commanded the colossal elephant to kneel her front legs down, allowing her and the shaman to slide down to the sand. "I bet you weren't expecting us to arrive so soon, Brother."

Bek slapped himself on the cheek. "Not with . . . all these . . . I mean, I knew you'd bring home a creature, but who are all these strangers? Who is the woman?"

"They're Pelasgians of the Deer Clan, who have been hiding in the hills for ages. And this is their shaman, Zugutan."

"We agreed to help, in exchange for a new home she promised us," Zugutan said. "It's right where your old colony used to stand."

Bek was taken aback. Why hadn't Itaweret run that offer by him first? "You mean you're going to settle at Per-Pehu . . . I hadn't expected anyone but us and our people to go back to Per-Pehu, but . . . I cannot say I object. Once we free the rest of our people, I suppose we could use some extra help in rebuilding our city."

He opened his palms in front of him, in a welcoming gesture. "Feel free to live among us!"

Zugutan blinked and looked at Itaweret with a disappointed frown. "Wait a moment, you want us to live *among* your people? I thought you told me we'd have the land all to ourselves, without any strange people to bother us. I hope that's what you said . . ."

Triopas stepped up. "No offense, but we certainly wouldn't want to move into a city with your people anyway, Itaweret. I've heard those places are crammed with thousands of people and stink to the highest heavens."

"Well, then you wouldn't have to live in the city with the Kemetians," Philos said. "There's plenty of countryside around it. I should know. I used to live there. Why not set up your little village on those outskirts?"

Zugutan shook her head, her arms crossed tight. "But there would still be Kemetians close by. Who knows how their descendants would treat us? They'd probably turn out no better than the Trojans. I'm sorry, but they'd have to go if we are to live in peace."

Bek threw up his arms. "Well, that's great, then. Sister, are you seriously going to bargain away our home to these primitive . . . strangers? Where are our people going to live? Are we going to swap places with them in those rugged valleys east of here?"

"Your people came from the land called Kemet, didn't they?" Zugutan said. "Why not simply return to the home of your ancestors?"

"We can't. The northernmost part of the kingdom has been taken over by the Hyksos, people from the east. We've been cut off from our mother country ever since."

"Maybe the Hyksos wouldn't mind us sailing through their territory if we're only going to rejoin our brethren to the south?" Itaweret asked. "It's not like we plan to attack them or anything."

"There's another issue, Sister." Bek glanced at Itaweret angrily. "My thinking is that, once we returned to Per-Pehu and rebuild it, I will reign as their great chief much as our father did. On the other hand, if we are simply to rejoin our kin in the motherland, we'd be obeying the pharaoh. And I wouldn't get to rule squat!"

Itaweret looked at everyone, and then shook her head. "So the problem is really your sense of pride, Brother."

Bek pointed his finger at Itaweret like a sword aimed at her heart. "It's not only pride! All my life, our father raised me to take his place as leader of the colony. If we have no colony, whom do I get to lead? What will my life's training be worth? By the gods, all our senet games together would have been for nothing!"

He sunk to his knees and pounded the sand with his fist. To see her younger brother so angry and distressed made Itaweret's heart sink like a heavy stone. She should have thought of something else to buy the Pelasgians' cooperation. Instead, she denied her brother the one thing he had aspired to achieve most in life. She shook her head, fighting back tears of anger. Toward herself. How could she have been so thoughtless?

Then she thought of the Deer Clan, how they took her offer, and were apparently so unwilling to budge an inch from something that wasn't even theirs yet. Why couldn't they be more flexible and allow the people of Per-Pehu to coexist with them? She also thought of Zugutan's point about how they would get along. Not well at all. She made a good point. The colony had always dealt with tension when it came to the native Achaeans, so it was indeed possible that a future great chief would prey on the Pelasgians the way their forefathers had fought with the Achaean tribes.

There was no easy way around this problem. How to please both her brother and Zugutan's clan?

An idea popped into Nebta's head. "Why not build a city of your own *within* Kemet, Bek? Maybe the pharaoh would appoint you as its chieftain then. He should be more than happy to have one more city in his domain to provide taxes for him."

"There isn't enough room in Kemetian territory for another settlement," Bek said. "Then what should I do?"

"How about we worry about all of this after we beat Scylax?" Itaweret said. "We need to focus on the present and concern ourselves with the future later."

Bek shrugged. "So be it. But I don't know if I'll ever forgive you for what you've done to me."

His words stabbed Itaweret sharper than any Mycenaean spear ever could. She turned away and walked over to Dedyet, resting herself against the elephant's warm foreleg while holding the scepter of Mut close to her body. Her heart and stomach felt as if something had been torn away from her for good. It had all been her fault. What to do?

Follow her own advice. *Better to focus on the present than worry about what would happen in the distant future.* There was an upcoming battle to win.

"While we're waiting for Scylax and his men to show up, we need to get away from this shoreline," Itaweret said. "They can't know we're here yet. Unless the Trojans change their minds, the only way we can beat the Mycenaeans is to ambush them."

"I like your thinking," Bek said, refocusing his anger into their immediate needs. "But where would we hide?"

"I don't know. Somewhere in the hills, I guess. How about we scout for a position soon?"

A nervous rumble arose from Dedyet, who spread her ears outward and raised the tip of her trunk to the sky. High overhead, a winged creature soared in wide circles while staring down with eyes burning bright silver. It let out a couple of echoing, screech-like hoots before swooping away into the cover of the clouds.

The air around Itaweret grew colder. She shook her head. "I think they already know where we are."

CHAPTER TWENTY-SIX

S cylax watched the heavens from the stern of his galley, the foremost of a fleet powered by the tireless rowing of enslaved Kemetian men. The slaves' muscles bunched and rippled beneath their dark skins with every pull of the oars, while Mycenaean soldiers prodded their backs with spearpoints. The unending rumble of the drivers' drumbeats set the pace. Not long ago, the Mycenaeans themselves rowed the ship. The conquest of Per-Pehu relieved them of that responsibility by shifting it to their abundant supply of captives. Scylax's men would always thank him for that.

He grinned when the cry of his sister's monster pierced through the clouds, along with the whoosh of the air as it flapped its wings. It dove onto the ship's deck, and the entire vessel bounced on the waves upon impact. Turning its beaked head to the bow, the creature called out to Kleno.

"What does she say?" Scylax asked.

"Exactly what we suspected," his sister said. "The Kemetian and her friends are still hiding near Troy."

The creature of Athena chirped again, and Kleno's expression turned to a nervous frown.

"There's something else," she added. "It appears that they've summoned a monster of their own."

Scylax could not find words that match his surprise. The only reason the Kemetian wench and her allies would have their own monster is if they had anticipated the one he and Kleno were bringing. How could they have known? Who would have given that knowledge away to them?

"What kind of monster is it?" Scylax said.

"Some kind of elephant, much bigger than the regular kind," Kleno replied. "It also seems to be every bit as big, if not even bigger, than our beast."

"An elephant, you say? At least it cannot fly like ours can. Right?"

"That is true. The question is, while our monster may be able to dodge its attacks, could she topple over its massive body? We will have to see."

"My question is, why would they summon their own creature if they don't know about ours? Somebody must be giving hints to them. But whom?"

Kleno tilted her face up to the cloudy sky. "Maybe they have a god on their side, too. I know not whom. All I do know is that we should prepare for the worst."

"Fair enough. We shall see for ourselves how strong this other god really is. How does that sound to you, O gray-eyed Athena?"

The beast responded with an eager hiss, determination glinting in its eyes.

Itaweret tossed and rolled in her cot. No matter how many times she moved into a more comfortable position, she could not impel herself to sleep.

She tore herself away and tiptoed out of her tent, careful not to step on Philos while he dozed. Nobody else appeared to be active in the camp outside, at least as far as the moonlight and stars could reveal. Even Xiphos had curled into a ball like a house cat right beside the tent. Toward the far edge of the encampment, Zugutan and the other Pelasgians lay on Dedyet's flank, as if the resting elephant had become a gigantic, leathery pillow. A slight smile formed on Itaweret's lips at that cute little sight.

She strolled past the camp's entrance and leaned against the trunk of a palm tree. There was no longer any way she and her people could win. If Scylax and his minions knew where they were, if they had no place to run or hide, then they might as well concede defeat. But what would that mean for Itaweret and her people?

Philos approached Itaweret and held up a blanket from his cot. "Aren't you a bit cold out here by yourself?"

"We should surrender," she said. "We'll be outnumbered, even with Dedyet and Xiphos at our side. Scylax has found out our position. We can't win the battle by ourselves, no matter how hard we try."

"Itaweret, what's gotten into you? Surrender should be out of the question. Your people are in chains, and that illegitimate tyrant is out to burn the entire world down, remember? How could you of all people possibly think of giving up now?"

"Listen, I don't *want* to give up any more than you do. It's only that we have no choice. If, on the other hand, we were to surrender to him, so many lives would be spared. There would be no more carnage."

"What makes you say that? You know what Scylax is after. Not stopping him means the whole world as we know it sinks into eternal carnage! What happened to you, girl? This doesn't sound like the Itaweret I know. Why, it was only a few days ago when you acted so sure we could win!"

Itaweret squeezed her hands together while clenching her teeth. "All right, I'll be honest. I think I may have given away too much to the Pelasgians to get them to side with us. Without our home in Per-Pehu, what would *my* people be fighting for?"

"That's easy. Their freedom. You don't want them to live under slavery forever, do you? You can sort out the problem of where they will live later."

"So, what do you propose we do now, Philos? Beg the king of Troy for his help, despite what he told us earlier?"

Philos stamped his foot. "Yes! How about going back the moment Scylax arrives? Let him know, right before the king of Troy himself, that you wouldn't dare give yourself up to him. Maybe then the Trojans will take your side."

Itaweret looked back to the hill which carried the city of Troy and its gleaming walls. "I hope you turn out to be right."

CHAPTER TWENTY-SEVEN

Once he had stepped onto his palace's highest balcony and looked down at the distant coast before his city, King Alexandros of Troy shouted a curse in disbelieving shock.

There must have been eighty ships, or maybe even a hundred. All bore flags atop their masts, flags a deeper red than the rising sun. Glimmering rivers of men in bronze poured off the decks, all of them flowing straight for the road to Troy's western gate.

Alexandros turned to one of his pages. "Who are these people? And what are they doing here?"

"I don't know why they've come," the boy said. "But I believe they all fly the flag of Mycenae, one of the Achaean cities."

The king thought back to the two Kemetians who had come to his court after Mycenae had destroyed their colony, begging him to avenge them. Was the same fate going to befall his own city now? From what he had known of Scylax, it was unlikely that the Mycenaean king would show Troy any more mercy. If only Alexandros had anticipated this would happen!

"Let us have a word with their king," he said.

He went down to his audience chamber and took his seat upon the throne, his fingers drumming on the armrests with trepidation as he waited for the Mycenaean ruler's entrance. All his life, Alexandros had sought to keep the Trojan people safe from attack, keeping them as far away from any form of war or conflict as possible. Never had he expected that the threat would wash upon his shores one morning like this, despite everything he had done.

Or did those Kemetians have something to do with it?

A trumpet blared twice. Within moments, a contingent of Mycenaean soldiers trooped into the room. Their red-caped leader stamped one foot onto the dais before Alexandros's throne with head held high, not even pausing to bow, as was custom for a visiting ruler to do.

"You should show a bit more deference to me," Alexandros said. "This is *my* city."

"It won't be your city anymore if you don't cooperate with our demands," the Mycenaean said. "As you should know by now, I am Scylax of Mycenae. And I believe you have something of great value to me."

"If it's land or tribute you want, you're not getting the slightest piece of either from me. Especially not with that attitude."

"Don't act stupid before me, king of Troy. We know you've a couple of Kemetian troublemakers within your territory. Have you been hiding them from us?"

Alexandros stood up, his facial muscles tensed with determination. "As a matter of fact, I do know whom you're talking about. They came to me pleading for my aid against you, but I told them I wasn't getting involved in their mess. If they're still hanging around here, it's not because I'm protecting them. What do you want from them, anyway?"

"Well, if they've come to you already, you should be able to recall that one of them was a young woman named Itaweret. Having already conquered her city of birth, I seek to claim her as a . . . celebration of my victory."

"And that's what you will never have!" a woman spoke.

She strutted into the audience chamber from a side corridor. It was the same Kemetian girl who had come to Alexandros earlier. Standing close behind her was the Achaean peasant boy who had gotten in trouble with Hector and his guards.

"I must say, that is quite spectacular timing you've demonstrated, Itaweret of Per-Pehu," Scylax said. "How about we resolve this little disagreement without recourse to bloodshed on either side? You know the deal. Become my bride and this will all be over."

"Will you promise to free my people if I do so?" Itaweret said.

"I'm afraid I can't promise *that*. You cannot even begin to imagine how much prosperity that keeping such a large workforce is already producing for my people. Or perhaps you can. After all, you Kemetians were enslaving us Achaeans centuries before, were you not?"

"That's all in the past," the Achaean youth said. "How about this for a counteroffer? You free her people and leave her alone, and I won't have to avenge my father—as in, your elder brother!"

Scylax laughed. "Oh, look, if it isn't the proud son of the late Metrophanes himself. How in Zeus's name do you plan to avenge his death, boy? You don't even have an army."

"I don't know about that, O king of Mycenae," Alexandros said. "I don't know the whole story, but it sounds to me like you've usurped your own throne. I have no more interest in helping a man like you out than I do these other people. If anything, I have more sympathy for the latter."

"What is that I hear? A threat of war against me?"

"Don't you dare twist my words like that, Scylax! But, if you don't depart from my shores immediately, then I'm afraid I will indeed have to force you away."

Scylax thrust a finger toward Itaweret. "We're not going any-where until you turn that Kemetian wench—and her filthy shep-herd friend—over to me. If men must die over that, so be it!"

Alexandros sat back on his throne and combed his beard with his fingers. The Mycenaeans were fierce fighters, but his Trojans would be no less disciplined on the battlefield, even if he hadn't used them in battle as much as other rulers. "It appears we have our deal. You and I shall fight it out on the plain south of the city."

Alexandros looked toward Itaweret and Philos. "My army and I will do our best to defend you against these Mycenaeans on the battlefield. But if we lose, please understand that you will have no choice but to agree to his terms. I would recommend doing so, for your sake."

Itaweret nodded. "Understood."

"That assumes he'll have any chance of beating us," Philos said. "Mark my words, Uncle Scylax, our combined forces will crush you into the red slime you deserve to become!"

The king of Mycenae crossed his brawny arms with a wide smirk. "I admire your valor, my young nephew. We shall see whether you'll carry it over into the big battle."

"Believe me, he will," Itaweret said. "As will I."

She and Philos withdrew from the throne chamber into the corridor.

CHAPTER TWENTY-EIGHT

The horns of war moaned the moment daylight poured onto the plain outside of Troy.

Perched on Dedyet's neck, Itaweret clutched the scepter of Mut with both hands as she and her allies watched the Trojans assemble from a summit overlooking the field. Several thousand spearmen gathered into a thick, straight line that faced westward. They held their shields up to form an armored wall. The famous Trojan chariots sped past both sides of the formation, manned by men with lances, clouds of dust streaming behind them into the air.

From the opposite end of the plain, the roaring army of Mycenae advanced toward the Trojans in an enormous concave formation, looking for all the world like a vast bronze monster ready to engulf its prey. Not good. Itaweret had always assumed the Trojan force would be a match for the Mycenaeans, yet the truth before her was that Scylax's men outnumbered Alexandros's by a significant factor. At least three to one. Even if their chariots managed to reach and harass the enemy's flanks for a while, the Trojans stood little chance of slaying the Mycenaean giant alone. They would be trampled into the grass.

Still, something seemed to be missing. For all the soldiers Scylax commanded on that plain, where were his sister and their monster?

Itaweret turned to Zugutan. "The Trojans don't have nearly enough men. Quick, can you conjure something up to cut down the Mycenaeans' numbers?"

"I will try. But be warned, I don't have much experience with spell-casting."

The Pelasgian shaman held up her arms to the scarlet-red sky and rolled her eyes back while chanting guttural lyrics in her native language. Silver-ringed strand by strand, her hair lifted and waved on end as her singing grew louder and more frenzied.

On the plain below, the Trojans and Mycenaeans began smashing into one another. The Trojan chariots rolled through the sides of the enemy's formation, leaving behind trails of crushed armor and bloodied flesh, but it did not take long for them to slow down and get caught and clogged in the thick melee. Zugutan needed to hurry up.

Overhead, dark purple-gray clouds emerged within the reddish sky. They expanded and coalesced into a titanic mass, casting the entire plain into shadow. The shaman's chanting blurred into howling growls like those of a rabid wolf, and the whites of her eyes gave off a scorching bright-white light while the wind twirling around her pulled at her levitating hair.

From the bottom of the giant cloud, a forked branch of lightning streaked into the middle of the Mycenaeans. Thunder boomed while chunks of burnt earth and bodies flung up into the air from the point of contact.

More lightning assailed the Mycenaeans. Between the newly formed craters, the cohesive wave of armored soldiers that marched onto the plain were being broken up and reduced into scurrying, screaming chaos. Panicking men ran in all directions and crashed into one another while the Trojans hacked away at their dissolved ranks, yelling with emboldened bloodlust.

As gory as the scene was, arms and heads being lopped off all over the field, Itaweret could not resist a smile curling up the corner of her mouth. This looked like it was going to be easier than she had expected.

Her smile turned into a frown. Perhaps *too* easy?

The storm cloud dissipated faster than it had appeared in the first place. Zugutan lolled about, the otherworldly light fading from her eyes, and rolled off the elephant's back.

Nebta hurried to catch the shaman in her arms. Laying Zugutan's motionless body on the ground, she pressed on her chest and breathed into her mouth. "The fall has knocked her out!"

On the plain, the scattered Mycenaeans pulled together and resumed their attack on the Trojans, their numbers so massive they still were able to encircle them despite suffering heavy losses. Even from a distance, the clangor of bashing shields and clashing bronze was terrific.

"Bek, lead the sailors and the Pelasgians to ambush them from behind!" Itaweret shouted. "The rest of us will have to join the battle from the side—"

A wide shadow cast darkness over her, and a shrieking roar drowned out everything else she could hear.

The sweep of the flying beast's feathered wings rammed Itaweret with a gust of wind that almost blew her off Dedyet's back. The giant scythe-like talons perched on its forelegs and tore the scepter of Mut out of Itaweret's grasp, snapping it in half like a mere stick. The claws of its hind legs ripped the skin on Dedyet's forehead until the elephant slapped it away with her trunk.

This new creature was what the eastern peoples called a griffin. At least, that was the closest beast Itaweret could find to describe it. It had the wings, head, and claws of an owl, yet its hindquarters resembled a lion. It outmatched a rhinoceros in sheer size.

After faltering in the air from the blow it had taken, the griffin dove for another attack with talons outstretched. Dedyet reared up on her back legs and bobbed her tusked head with a threatening trumpet. There the two beasts crashed into one another, the force of which threw Itaweret off. It was Philos who caught her before she could hit the ground.

Gore sputtered everywhere as griffin and elephant wrestled each other on the hilltop. Claws sliced over wrinkled hide while tusks stabbed into feathered flesh. Underneath them, the earth quaked with every stomp of their feet.

The griffin tore itself away from the strangling grasp of Dedyet's trunk and chomped off the tip with its beak. The elephant reeled with a shrill, wailing trumpet until she toppled over. Itaweret heard her ribs crack as she collided with the ground.

Xiphos roared mightily and pounced toward the griffin. It batted him away with its foreleg. Nebta slung her bow and fired an arrow at the creature, but it evaded her missile while launching itself at Itaweret. It grabbed Itaweret by the forearm and carried her off into the sky.

The world shrank fast beneath Itaweret's dangling feet. Her friends on the hilltop became tiny as ants, the fallen elephant appearing no larger than a mouse. After the griffin flapped its wings to propel through the air, everything around her blended into a giant blur. She squirmed and screamed against the monster's clutches, dreading that it would bite her head off. That did not happen. Instead, the griffin soared over the landscape to another hill adjoining the coast and descended to its surface with a rapid plunge. There, it dropped Itaweret onto an outcropping that lay flat like an altar, with Kleno standing over it.

The Mycenaean priestess cackled. "You thought you could slip away from my brother and me so easily, didn't you? Yet in the end, not even your tame elephant could save you."

"What do you want this time?" Itaweret asked. "If you want to kill me, all you need to do is order your overgrown pet bird to finish me off."

"Why would I want to kill you? I've been hunting you down on my brother's behalf, haven't I? Truth be told, I have even greater use for you. What I need, Itaweret of Per-Pehu, is a loyal acolyte. An apprentice and a successor if you will."

"Why, by all the gods, would I want to serve you?"

"You want to get rid of Scylax, don't you? The best way you can do that is by joining me. Together, we can remove him and seize control of Mycenae for ourselves. In fact, I might even let you have the throne all to yourself. What say you to that?"

As if things could not get any stranger . . .

Itaweret was at a loss for words. Had Kleno been plotting to betray her own brother this entire time? Was she seriously offering Itaweret an opportunity to defeat him, or was this some sort of deception? It sounded far too good to be true.

Still, something about the prospect of ruling Mycenae appealed to Itaweret in a strange way. From that throne, she could undo all the damage Scylax had caused, except for her fellow citizens that he had slaughtered already, and forge the Mycenaeans into a more peaceful nation that no longer posed a threat to anyone. She might even give the people of Per-Pehu the one thing she wanted them to have more than anything else in the world.

"You have to promise that I can free my people as queen of Mycenae," Itaweret said firmly.

"You mean the people of Per-Pehu?" Kleno asked. "Why would you want to do that? Do you not realize the great amount of wealth having such a numerous workforce could bring us?"

"They are my people! If I cannot free them, then to the depths of the underworld with your offer!"

The smile evaporated from Kleno's face. "Very well. Athena, or should I say, *Sennuwy*, destroy the Kemetian girl who used to be your friend!"

The griffin's front talons squeezed tight around Itaweret's waist. They were not friends now. As the creature lifted her to its open beak, Itaweret hammered her fists onto its fingers with frantic desperation. The avian monster's hot rancid breath overwhelmed her sense of smell to the point of drowning out her consciousness. She lay on the brink of passing out before the griffin had closed its beak on her flesh. She used what remained of her strength to punch the beast in the face and rip out a tuft of its feathers.

After the griffin released her and let out a shrieking exclamation of agony, Itaweret sprinted down the hill to a patch of rose bushes and crouched behind them. She tore out a handful of the plants' thorny stems and brandished them as the creature leaped after her. They cut a series of gashes across the palms of the griffin's front feet.

Again she swung the bundle of stems, but the beast's beak snapped onto them and yanked them away. With one foreleg, the griffin pinned her onto the earth with crushing force while lowering its open, drool-leaking beak to her head.

With an elephantine trumpet, Dedyet rammed into the monster's side and shoved it away from Itaweret.

Dedyet had returned to fight with the shaman Zugutan mounted on her. The elephant grabbed the griffin by the neck and coiled around it with her trunk, snapping the neck vertebrae underneath. The gagging feathered predator struggled to claw its way out of Dedyet's grasp until the latter threw it onto the upper lip of a cliff hanging over the sea. With more kicks of her stout and solid legs, the elephant sent Kleno's monster plummeting onto the sharp rocks at the bottom. The griffin's blood-soaked corpse exploded into a giant ball of silver light that then shrank into nothingness.

Zugutan jumped down from Dedyet's back and handed Itaweret the two halves of the scepter of Mut. "See if you can finish that Mycenaean she-demon off with these."

Itaweret held the two pieces of metal together. They reattached to one another at the ends and melded together with scintillating gold light. "I will be more than happy to."

"Oh no, you don't, you sooty bitch!"

Kleno threw herself at Itaweret like a pouncing lioness, but Itaweret had little trouble dodging her. She raised the scepter of Mut high over the Mycenaean priestess's body and swung its tip down onto her skull, breaking it open.

"Damn you to Hades, you nappy-headed Kemetian whore!" Kleno screamed as her consciousness receded quickly. "May all your people suffer in chains forever! May all you melanchroides . . ."

Rivers of gold vapor hissed up from her body as it dissolved into oblivion. Not even her wolf-skin shawl remained. Kleno, high priestess of Athena in Mycenae, was no more, exactly like the creatures she had commanded in life.

Brushing blood and perspiration off her brow, Itaweret turned to Zugutan. "I thought you got knocked out?"

"I didn't take that long to recover," Zugutan said. "Once I did, I used a little of my power to heal Dedyet and lead her to where you were taken. Now, let's go join the others in smashing Scylax's ass, shall we?"

CHAPTER TWENTY-NINE

The coppery smell of blood, spilled organs, and singed flesh polluted the air. Bek and Nebta stole through a row of olive trees along the plain's western boundary. Before them, the bodies of slain and trampled men and horses created a vast carpet over the battlefield, with a layer of gore slicked over the grass. Hazy smoke from Zugutan's lightning strikes stung his eyes to the point of drawing tears.

Further away to the east, the battle between Mycenae and Troy raged on. Scylax's forces stretched between the horizons, a long and thick fence of fighting men. Even after their partial decimation by the lightning storm, they still were far more numerous than the crew of unarmored Phoenician sailors with scimitars who followed Bek and Nebta. How could such a paltry mob possibly overcome all those bronze-clad professionals?

Bek heard the rustle of leaves and pounding crackle of twigs coming toward him. He held his dagger up, his heart thumping at a panicked rate. With a downward wave of his arm, he gestured to his army to lie low and still.

A sweaty, sienna-brown–skinned man with a thick fluffy beard and corded musculature on his arms burst through the bushes ahead. His linen loincloth, though tattered and soiled with mud, betrayed a Kemetian heritage. Running toward Bek, the man threw up his arms and hollered praises to all the gods for his good fortune.

"Thank goodness you're alive, son of Mahu!" the man said. He looked at Nebta and the Phoenicians. "What are you doing with these strangers?"

"Leading a rear ambush against the Mycenaeans," Bek answered. "Now who would you be?"

"Call me Tjenna. I, along with so many of our countrymen, have been forced to row the ships that brought those Achaean jackals here. When we spotted you and your army moving along the shore, we thought you would break us free of our bondage."

"Of course, somebody like Scylax would use slave labor to row his fleet," Nebta said. "Look at you. You look like you've been dragged through the dark bowels of the earth!"

"If Scylax has been using my people as galley slaves, he'll regret doing so," Bek said. "Bring me to your mates, Tjenna."

He and Tjenna ran to the shore where the Mycenaean galleys were beached. Between them and the ships, a dense throng of Kemetian men in rags sat or lay on the beach, exhausted beyond measure, their weary eyes locked on Bek. Their ribs poked through the skin on their torsos, as if they had not eaten a real meal in weeks. The arms and backs of many were striped with dark-purple scars, and they gave off an overpowering stench of sweat and human dung. To see the proud men of Per-Pehu in such an abused condition soured Bek's mood, but it did not damper his hunger for battle.

Instead, it kindled it further.

"Men of Per-Pehu, today shall be the day you gain your freedom back," Bek told them. "Never again shall you answer to the whip and spear of the Mycenaean oppressors who have destroyed your city and raped your sisters and daughters. I, the son of Mahu, have returned to lead you to liberation. Together, we shall slaughter the demons of Mycenae as a pride of lions against antelope. May Sekhmet and Horus grant us strength and courage today!"

He raised his fist to the air. The men of Per-Pehu did the same in unison, hooting battle cries while stamping their feet like war drums. In their hands were broken halves of their oars, which they snapped over their knees with a renewed strength and then waved like spears.

Bek led the men back to the trees, where Nebta and her crew awaited them. Together they sneaked onto the plain in a wide line toward the Mycenaeans' rear. Picking up a spear and shield from one of the dead soldiers on the field, Bek sped into a gallop as he drew closer to the enemy. Every pulse of his heart drove him faster.

Next to him, Nebta fished out her bow and shot into the Mycenaean ranks. A man screamed as her arrow hit the exposed nape of his neck.

"Charge!"

Bek's men roared as they heeded his command and threw themselves at the enemy from the rear. With unbridled fury, he thrust, stabbed, and slashed about with the spear he had stolen, washing himself with the blood spurting from the skulls and necks of the slain enemy. Encumbered by their clunky suits of armor, the Mycenaean soldiers were slow to turn around and retaliate. Once you knew where to strike, it was so easy that it was almost disappointing.

Then a Mycenaean sword chopped through the shaft of Bek's spear. Twirling on his feet away from his assailant's reach, Bek took out his dagger and flung it into the Mycenaean's brow. Now he had only his hands and feet to defend himself. Time to make the most of it. Bek spun and sprung his way through the chaos, knocking and pushing the barbarians in bronze away from him with punches, kicks, and strikes of his elbows and knees.

His fists and kicks stopped when the keen edge of another Mycenaean blade cleaved through his right shoulder. The gory stump that remained shot extreme, crippling pain through his body. As his strength drained away, images of the gods judging him for entry into the afterlife haunted Bek's imagination.

Another of Nebta's arrows ripped through the eye of the Mycenaean, taking him out. She hauled the wounded Bek onto her shoulder and wove in a hurry through the thick melee, maneuvering around the blows of enemy and ally alike.

Once they had exited the battle, she put him down beneath the protective shade of an olive tree. "I'll go get something to stop your bleeding. Rest here."

Bek moaned. "We're going to lose, aren't we?"

Nebta kissed him on the cheek. "Oh, don't worry. We are already close to winning. See how well we're doing?"

He looked up. She was right. The sailors and liberated oarsmen continued cutting and stabbing away at the Mycenaean rear, with none routed yet as far as Bek could see.

Then, amid the distant din of carnage, a lion's roar.

Spinning his shepherd's staff overhead, Philos penetrated the fray from the side. Behind him, Triopas and his Pelasgian tribesmen assaulted the Mycenaeans with cudgels and spears. The crude, stone-headed weapons appeared surprisingly effective in denting the soldiers' armor and butchering them, he thought. Xiphos's leonine strength, claws, and fangs were taking a toll of their own, the feline's swiftness keeping lion and master out of reach of Mycenaean counterattacks.

Philos himself had little interest in the butchery. When the battle was done, these Mycenaeans would become his own people. There was only one among them that he was hungry to slay—the man that stood between him and what was rightfully his own, the man who had displaced his father and then had him killed, along with everyone else Philos had grown up with. The man responsible for everything miserable in Philos's life.

"There you are, son of Metrophanes!"

With his red cape flowing behind him in the wind, Scylax of Mycenae loomed tall over Philos, his blood-splattered breastplate gleaming in the sunlight like the ember hide of an underworld demon. His eyes glinted with murderous glee as he drew his sword for the kill.

Philos swung his staff onto Scylax's sword-arm. The staff broke into two, but Scylax did not drop his weapon as hoped.

He laughed. "You're going to have to do better than that, little nephew!"

Scylax slashed a deep gash across Philos's chest. Crumpling onto the ground, Philos raced to pick up the two halves of his staff. He managed to grab one before Scylax stepped on it and kicked him in the jaw. "I must say I'm underwhelmed," he said. "I'd thought you'd put up more of a fight."

"Why did you dethrone my father?" Philos asked. "He would have been a better king than you."

"Your father was weak. I wanted our kingdom to be strong. And strong it shall be!"

"No, you'll make our kingdom *weaker*. Look around you. Your own men are dying before you on three fronts. Don't you see? War makes them weak."

"Silence, boy!"

"You are a weak king, Scylax! You're nothing more than an overgrown bully. You can have as many of your own men killed as you want, but you will never be as strong as my father."

Now growling with rage, Scylax hacked down at Philos, who rolled out of the way. The tip of the king's sword buried deep into the gore-dampened earth. As Scylax struggled to pull it out, Philos retrieved the upper half of his staff and whacked the tyrant of Mycenae on the back, knocking him down.

Philos whistled while pulling off the helmet from Scylax's head. "Xiphos! You can have him."

The lion leapt and sank his red-stained fangs into Scylax's neck. The cruel king yelled out the most profane curses at Philos until his voice gave way to a croaking death rattle.

Scylax, the treacherous brother of Metrophanes, and the cruel slaving warlord of Mycenae, was bound for the darkest depths of the underworld.

"Say hello to my father for me on your way to Tartarus," Philos whispered under his breath.

An elephantine bray sounded over the carnage. Philos heard the crumple of metal, the crunching of bone, and the screams of men as Dedyet trampled through what remained of the Mycenaean ranks. He also heard the whooping war cries of Itaweret and Zugutan as they rode her. Joining the pair in their triumphant hollering were the Trojans, Pelasgians, Phoenicians, Kemetians, and all allies in the battle. Philos yelled praises to Ares for the strength that the god of war had bestowed upon all of them.

By Zeus and all the other gods on Mount Olympus, the battle had been won.

Their numbers now whittled away to a tiny fraction of what they were when the battle began, the men of Mycenae dropped their weapons and fled toward the north, their enemies hollering taunts at them.

A wave of triumphant roars swept over the battlefield as all the Trojans and their allies brandished their weapons and banged their shields with them.

Dedyet trotted over to Philos and knelt on her front legs. Itaweret extended an arm toward him and pulled him onto the elephant's back between her and Zugutan.

"What happened to the griffin?" Philos asked.

Zugutan patted the skin on the elephant's back. "Suffice to say, she and her mistress are no more."

Bek and Nebta approached next, Nebta holding a reddened wad of cloth over the spot where Bek's right arm should have been.

Itaweret's eyes opened wide. "By holy Mut, what happened to you, Brother?"

"Don't worry, I'll be alright," Bek said. "Men have lived through much worse wounds. The important thing is, we won."

CHAPTER THIRTY

Drums rumbled, their rhythm upbeat, as lyres twanged and an ensemble of singers chanted joyous lyrics within King Alexandros's spacious dining hall. The appetizing fragrance of roast boar floated from the spit that two Trojans rotated over the room's central hearth, mingling with the sweeter smells of fresh fruit and wine, which servants distributed from platters and pitchers. The hearth's fire bathed the room in a warm, cozy orange light, driving away the darkness beneath a star-dusted sky.

Alexandros raised his drinking cup and spoke in his loudest voice. "Before we continue the feast, I would like to state my thanks to all the gods of Troy for our great victory against Scylax of Mycenae. Not only that, but I also owe a portion of my gratitude to all our allies who fought beside us: the liberated Kemetians of Per-Pehu, the valiant warriors of the Pelasgian Deer Clan, and the hardy sailors under Captain Nebta. Without their invaluable aid, we could not have accomplished what we did, and instead would have been forced into submission to Mycenaean tyranny. A round of applause to all our benefactors, please!"

Everyone clapped and cheered with a noisy jubilation.

"In honor of all the foreign aid we have received, I would like to announce a revision of our policies toward all the people who come to our city seeking refuge," Alexandros went on. "We need to show much more hospitality toward them from now on. No longer shall we force them to camp outside our walls in a state of squalor. Instead, we shall do everything in our power to welcome them and treat them as our equals, as fellow citizens of Troy. The time has come to put away our prejudices and embrace unity through diversity!"

The room echoed from the next wave of applause.

Itaweret helped herself to a little wine and smacked her lips. It seemed an entire lifetime had passed since she had enjoyed the food and drink of luxury. Her hostess, the Trojan queen, had been kind enough to let her female servants dress up Itaweret in the purest white linen gown and most exquisite gold jewelry to replace what she had lost and soiled over the course of the journey and battle. For a moment, Itaweret felt as though she had come home to Per-Pehu in its glory days.

Next to her, Zugutan spit out a mouthful of wine and tossed the cup away. "How can you possibly drink this sour filth? It's the most revolting thing I have ever tasted!"

Nebta chortled. "I take it you're not a fan of the finer things in life, my Pelasgian friend."

Bek wrapped his one arm around Nebta's waist and kissed her on the cheek. The Trojan healers had wrapped up the stump with thick linen bandages. It would take Itaweret a long while to get used to seeing her brother in that condition, even though he seemed to be recovering with a miraculous swiftness.

"Where do you plan on going from here, Brother?" Itaweret asked.

Bek looked at Nebta and nodded. "We've decided to lead the people of Per-Pehu back to Kemet. After hearing of our victory against the Mycenaeans, the pharaoh should reward me handsomely. Maybe he'll make me a general in his army?"

Nebta returned Bek's kiss. "And I'll get to be your lieutenant, won't I?"

"Not only that, my dear." He gave her a wink and a grin.

"If your people are leaving Per-Pehu for good, does that mean my clan can move in there?" Zugutan asked. "To fulfill the offer made by Itaweret?"

"Precisely. It's all yours, Zugutan of the Deer Clan."

"I know where I'll be going in the meantime," Itaweret said.

She sauntered over to a column against which Philos leaned and handed over a leg of boar to Xiphos. Philos was not smiling from the victory like everyone else in the room. If anything, his frown conveyed a sense of worry. "You don't look like you're having that good a time," Itaweret said. "May I ask why?"

"I guess . . . I'm a bit nervous. I'm going to be the king of Mycenae, after fighting in this big battle against my own people. That's quite a burden to carry on my shoulders."

Itaweret wrapped her arms around him and shook her hip slightly, catching his eye, as she'd intended. "Don't worry. I will be ruling beside you as your queen. Now, why don't you and I head on over to our bedchamber?"

Philos chuckled. "Isn't that a delightful way to end the party for both of us?"

Itaweret planted her lips on Philos, and they shared a long kiss. From the corner of her eye, she noticed a beam of golden light entering one of the windows in the hall's outer wall. She peered over Philos's shoulder to behold the goddess Mut, floating in the light.

Mut gave her a gentle smile. "Well done, my priestess."

CHARACTER ARTWORK

For full-color artwork and more behind-the-scenes info about
Priestess of the Lost Colony,
visit brandonpilchersart.com/my-books.

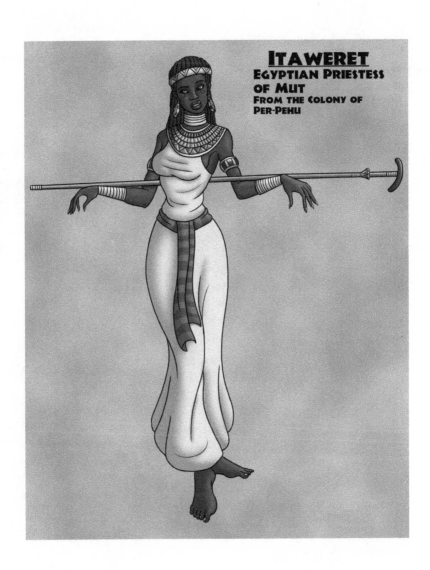

ITAWERET
EGYPTIAN PRIESTESS
OF MUT
FROM THE COLONY OF
PER-PEHU

BEK
KEMETIAN COLONIAL PRINCE
FROM THE COLONY OF PER-PEHU

PHILOS
ACHAEAN SHEPHERD
FROM THE VILLAGE OF
TAUROCEPHALUS
HAS A TAME LION NAMED
XIPHOS

SCYLAX
KING OF MYCENAE

KLENO
PRIESTESS
OF ATHENA
FROM THE CITY-STATE
OF MYCENAE